DOC SAVAGE'S AMAZING CREW

William Harper Littlejohn, the bespectacled scientist who was the world's greatest living expert on geology and archaeology.

Colonel John Renwick, "Renny," his favorite sport was pounding his massive fists through heavy, paneled doors.

Lieutenant Colonel Andrew Blodgett Mayfair, "Monk," only a few inches over five feet tall, and yet over 260 pounds. His brutish exterior concealed the mind of a great scientist.

Major Thomas J. Roberts, "Long Tom," was the physical weakling of the crowd, but a genius at electricity.

Brigadier General Theodore Marley Brooks, slender and waspy, he was never without his ominous, black sword cane.

WITH THEIR LEADER, THEY WOULD GO ANYWHERE, FIGHT ANYONE, DARE EVERYTHING—SEEKING EXCITEMENT AND PERILOUS ADVENTURE!

Bantam Books by Kenneth Robeson

THE MAN OF BRONZE
THE THOUSAND-HEADED MAN
METEOR MENACE
THE POLAR TREASURE
BRAND OF THE WEREWOLF
THE LOST OASIS
THE MONSTERS
THE LAND OF TERROR
THE MYSTIC MULLAH
THE PHANTOM CITY
FEAR CAY
QUEST OF QUI
LAND OF ALWAYS-NIGHT
THE FANTASTIC ISLAND
MURDER MELODY
THE SPOOK LEGION
THE RED SKULL
THE SARGASSO OGRE
PIRATE OF THE PACIFIC
THE SECRET IN THE SKY
COLD DEATH
THE CZAR OF FEAR
FORTRESS OF SOLITUDE
THE DEVIL'S PLAYGROUND
DEATH IN SILVER
THE MYSTERY UNDER THE SEA
THE DEADLY DWARF
THE GREEN EAGLE
THE OTHER WORLD
THE ANNIHILIST
THE FLAMING FALCONS
DUST OF DEATH

DUST
OF DEATH

A DOC SAVAGE ADVENTURE
BY KENNETH ROBESON

DUST OF DEATH

A Bantam Book / published by arrangement with
The Condé Nast Publications Inc.

PRINTING HISTORY
Originally published in DOC SAVAGE *Magazine October 1935*
Bantam edition published January 1969

Bantam Books are published by Bantam Books, Inc., a subsidiary
of Grosset & Dunlap, Inc. Its trade-mark, consisting of the words
"Bantam Books" and the portrayal of a bantam, is registered in the
United States Patent Office and in other countries. Marca Registrada.
Bantam Books, Inc., 271 Madison Avenue, New York, N.Y. 10016.

PRINTED IN THE UNITED STATES OF AMERICA

Chapter 1

THE COMING OF TROUBLE

THE PLANE slammed down for a landing in a way that stood the hair on end, and conveyed the thought that the pilot did not care much for his life. The ship sank out of the South American sky in a power dive that made a moan which could be heard for miles. It hauled out, went into a side-slip that seemed more than a ship could stand. Then it landed.

The landing told things. The pilot was neither reckless nor a fool. He was a wizard.

The man who got out of the plane looked as if he were about ready to die. Not that he was wounded, not that he had any affliction. He was just a pale bag of bones, and not a very large bag. His complexion was about as inviting as green bananas.

The man peered about. Then, quite suddenly, he shoved a hand inside his greasy flying suit.

The flying field was jittery with heat waves. The fighting planes—very modern military planes they were—over by the army hangars were like baked insects that had just crawled out of hangars that were ovens.

Trouble was coming from the hangars in the shape of a squad of uniformed brown soldiers. There was trained precision in their advance, even if they were in a hurry. Their faces were grim and their rifles clean—cocked.

The officer in charge of the squad was dapper, efficient, and, coming up to the flyer who had the look of an invalid, he presented a blue automatic, muzzle first. He spoke brisk and grim Spanish.

"This is a military airport, señor," he said. "No landings are permitted here. You are under arrest."

"*Si, si, amigo,*" said the puny-looking flyer.

He took his hand out of his flying suit and it held papers, official looking. He passed them over.

The officer took them and read them, and his eyebrows went up, then down, and his shoulders did the same. He spoke English this time and it was not especially good.

"Our consul, he ees not have right for you thees military field to use," he said. "Eet ees not what you call—call——"

1

"Not regular, I know," said the flyer. "But suppose you call your chief, contact some one high up in the war department. I did a little telephoning before I started."

The officer did tricks with his eyebrows while he thought that over.

"I will see," he said. "You wait."

He took the papers, which the flyer had given him, and walked away briskly, going past the hangars and along the walk which led to the operations office.

The officer took quick strides, eying from time to time the documents which obviously held great interest for him. He shook his head, sucked his tongue, and spoke to himself.

"If this flyer's identity is as these papers say," he murmured, "it means great and amazing things are to come."

He turned a corner briskly. The path, virtually an alley, ran between thick walls of shrubbery on either side.

"If this man is who these say he is," the officer waved papers at himself, "the mystery of the Inca in Gray may be solved after all."

A man came out of the bushes into the path behind the officer. He came swiftly without much noise.

The man was bent over and his hands were across his middle as if he had a permanent pain there. A beggar, to judge by his looks. His hair was long. His *poncho* ragged, his fiber sandals frayed. Unless the matter was given thought, it might not occur that the fellow was excellently disguised.

"Señor *soldado*," the ragamuffin hissed, "I have something to tell, important."

The officer stopped, turned and, surprised, let the tall, stooped bundle of rags come up to him. He was unsuspicious. In the South American republic of Santa Amoza civilians treated army officers with respect. Not being suspicious was the officer's mistake.

The ragamuffin had a knife concealed in his hand. But the officer did not see that until he looked down at his chest and saw the hilt sticking out over his heart. Queerly, the army man kept his mouth closed tightly. But, after a moment, strings of crimson leaked from the corners of his mouth, a string from each corner at almost the same time. Then the army officer, in a slow, horrible way, got down on his hands and knees and lay on the knife hilt so that the point was shoved on through, and the point came out of the back of his neat khaki uniform.

He kicked as he died.

2

THE KILLER was a thrifty soul. He got his knife. Then he got the papers. After which he scampered away through the brush, making as little noise as he could.

Beyond the flying field was jungle, where there was rainfall down here on the coast where sat Alcala, capital city of Santa Amoza. Once in the jungle, the slayer ran as if his shadow were a devil. After a time, he came to a house, a very miserable looking hovel and apparently untenanted, but which held a modern telephone.

The telephone set-up was remarkable. Not the instrument itself, which was ordinary, but the box of apparatus through which its circuit ran. The device was what is known as a "scrambler" and it was ordinarily employed by telephone companies on government lines where eavesdroppers were not wanted. Only the proper unscrambler at the other end would make intelligible what went over the wire.

"Word must be got to the Inca in Gray," said the killer. "The thing we feared has happened."

"What do you mean?" demanded a coarse voice.

They were speaking Spanish.

"Major Thomas J. Roberts just arrived at military field," snapped the slayer. "I thought I recognized him. I used my knife on a fool officer, and got diplomatic passes which prove the man is indeed Major Thomas J. Roberts."

"And who might Major Thomas J. Roberts be?" the voice over the wire demanded.

"Who was your father, my friend?" asked the killer.

"He was a man of Inca blood, of which I am proud," rapped the other. "And what has that to do——"

"I thought he must have been an ox," sneered the slayer, "for naught but an ox could sire a son so dumb. This man Roberts is more commonly known as Long Tom."

"And so what, insulting dog?" demanded the other. "Is this Long Tom *Señor Diablo* himself?"

"He is worse," declared the ragamuffin. "He is the assistant, one of the five assistants rather, of the one man our master, the Inca in Gray, fears."

"Continue, man of many words and little information," directed the voice on the wire.

"Doc Savage!" said the killer. "Long Tom is the assistant of Doc Savage."

There was silence. It was a long silence, as if the man on the other end of the wire had been hit a hard blow and was recovering. Then he began to swear, and his profanity was like the explosions of bundles of fire-crackers. He started in a loud scared voice and swore until he ran out of breath.

"Wait," he said.

3

The killer waited. It was all of five minutes. Then the other was back on the line.

"The Inca in Gray will direct this personally," he said. "This Long Tom will be disposed of."

"Good-by, son of an ox," the killer chuckled and hung up.

BACK AT the military flying field there was excitement. For the body of the knifed officer had been found. It was orderly excitement, grim. For these soldiers of Santa Amoza were well trained—and long trained, for the war had been going on for four years already.

"Long Tom" Roberts was in the office of the field commander, standing stark naked, for he had been stripped as they searched him. He looked more than ever like a man who was waiting for a coffin. But there was nothing moribund about the Spanish he spoke. It was good Spanish. He used plenty of it, pointedly, loudly.

"Call Señor Junio Serrato, war minister of Santa Amoza," Long Tom bellowed. "He'll okay me. He knows I'm coming."

They finally did call Señor Junio Serrato, war minister, and what he said must have been emphatic and plenty. For the flying field officials turned suddenly apologetic.

"My treatment of you is to be regretted greatly. But you must understand our country is at war," the field commander himself said. "And the mysterious murder of the officer——"

There was much shrugging, in the middle of which Long Tom Roberts left. He took a horse-drawn hack driven by an old woman who looked like the Yankee conception of a witch. All gasoline was commandeered for military use in Santa Amoza and all ablebodied men were in the army. Long Tom eventually got into town.

Alcala after the fashion of South American cities, was a bright-colored town, made brighter by the flags which hung in profusion. Bright sunshine made the white houses whiter and filled the streets with heat waves. Tourists would have ecstasized over the place.

But there were no tourists. There was war!

It showed in something besides the numbers of uniformed men. There was a grimness, chill in the faces, a thing as distinct as the snow-capped Andes, which could be distinctly seen inland.

Long Tom surrendered his conveyance, because marching squads of soldiers frequently held him up and he could make better time walking.

The walking, Long Tom concluded in short order, was a mistake. There were beggars; war makes beggars. Tattered and filthy and pleading, they tagged at his heels. He tossed

4

them coins, knowing that was a mistake, for it drew more of them like sugar in the midst of flies. He tossed more coins, but they grew bolder, more insistent. They scuttled alongside him, tugged his clothing.

The presence of the beggars was not strange, for tropical cities are commonly infested with mendicants.

But suddenly it was strange. It was sinister. It had a purpose.

One whining rogue, ragged and dirty as the rest, shuffled up, arms held loosely at his sides, bare feet scuffing the dust of the unpaved street. Then, unexpectedly, his long arms were wrapped around Long Tom's slight figure.

"Spy!" screamed the beggar. "He is a spy!"

The mob burst out in a roar. The suddenness with which it happened showed this all had been arranged. Unclean hands closed upon Long Tom. There seemed to be dozens of them.

"Spy!" they shrieked. "Kill him!"

"Kill him!" a score echoed.

Then Long Tom—he who resembled an invalid—picked up the first beggar who had seized him. Using the victim as a club, Long Tom bowled over fully half a dozen others. It was a feat the burliest wrestler would not have blushed to recount.

In the next few seconds, Long Tom demonstrated some of the qualities which qualified him as an assistant to that man whose name was legend to the far corners of the earth —Doc Savage. Long Tom used his fists at first, and they landed with noises only slightly less than pistol shots.

A ring opened around Long Tom, in it the bodies of those who had become senseless. The mob roared, circled the man whose mild appearance was so deceptive.

"Kill him!" it bawled. "A spy!"

Then they closed in, and many knives appeared. They tore a stoop from in front of a house, and hurled these sizable rock fragments. Long Tom got one in the chest and it put him down.

Lying there, gasping, he drove hands into his pockets. They came out with small glass bulbs. He broke these in the street, and they made wet splashes which vaporized away almost instantly. It was gas, odorless, producing quick unconsciousness if breathed—a product of Doc Savage's inventive genius. Long Tom held his breath so as not to get any of it. He got up and ran.

Into a door, Long Tom dived, not knowing where it led. He was lucky. It admitted into a patio, and he climbed a palm tree to a roof, crossed that, got into another street, after which it was doubtful if a man in the mob could have kept up with him. He could hear them yelling.

"Spy!" they screamed. "Kill him!"

"Whoever hatched that murder scheme," Long Tom grumbled as he ran, "was clever."

Chapter 2

THE GRAY DEAD

ALCALA, CAPITAL of Santa Amoza, had the outward aspects of a backward city and a poor one. It was neither. Santa Amoza was a country rich in natural resources—nitrates and oil among others—and before the war a flood of exports had poured out of Alcala, the seaport, and a flood of gold had poured in. Alcala had been a rich field for American salesmen.

The government hospital was a typical example of just how modern Alcala was. The building was huge, white and of fine stone. The interior was also white and sanitary, modern to the extreme.

Long Tom Roberts was following a stern-faced male nurse down a hall and into a big room, where a man lay on a white cot.

The man on the cot was a mummy in bandages, except for his hands and his face. He had an interesting face. At some time or other his nose had made forcible contact with an object harder than its tissue and bone. The nose gave the man a face remindful of the countenance of an English bulldog. Inside the bandages the man's frame was probably angular and capable.

The bandaged man did not see Long Tom at first.

Long Tom grinned and said: "All wrapped up for shipping."

The bandaged man turned over. His blue eyes all but came out of his head. He tried to bound out of the cot and fell on the floor.

"Long Tom!" he howled. "You old corpse, you old rascal, you sonuvagun!"

"Ace Jackson," Long Tom chuckled.

Long Tom helped him back on the cot, and they grinned and mauled each other a little, shouting things which did not make much sense.

"Ace Jackson," Long Tom chuckled. "Same old Kiwi. Haven't seen you since you were flying a Spad, back in the Great War."

"Same here," chortled "Ace" Jackson. "Swell of you to drop in to see me, you pint of dynamite."

"I was down in Argentina on a hydro-electric project,"

Long Tom explained. "Buzzed up here as soon as I heard that you had tried to do a bit of flying without wings. What's the idea? Been flying so long you thought you had sprouted wings?"

Ace Jackson looked suddenly grim and did not answer.

Long Tom stepped back and eyed the bandaged aviator uriously.

"It must have taken *some* sky battler to bring you down," he said dryly. "Did they gang you? I'll swear no one man could outfly you."

"The Inca in Gray may not be a man—I think sometimes," Ace Jackson said slowly and distinctly.

For the first time, Long Tom became aware there was a girl in the room. She was tall, dark haired. And her complexion had the utter fairness of the pure Castilian. She came forward when she saw that Long Tom had perceived her.

Long Tom had the sudden feeling that he was looking upon the most beautiful girl he had ever seen in his life.

Ace Jackson made introductions.

"This is Señorita Anita Carcetas, daughter of the president of this republic," he said. "Anita, I want you to meet Major Thomas J. Roberts, better known as Long Tom, electrical wizard extraordinary. And a lug who would rather fight than eat. And he loves his food. Where there's trouble you'll find Long Tom, and he's a pal of mine."

"I have not been so dazzled since I saw my first sunrise," Long Tom said gallantly.

His eyes told him things. These two were violently in love.

The girl was patting pillows, adjusting coverlets and bandages and otherwise making Ace Jackson comfortable. She was getting such a big kick out of it that Long Tom let her continue for a while. Then he spoke.

"You said something a moment ago," he reminded Ace Jackson.

The wounded flyer looked around the girl at him. "Eh?" he queried.

"The Inca in Gray," Long Tom explained.

Over Ace Jackson's face came an expression as if he had just met, face to face, a bitter and detested enemy.

"I guess it's a man," he muttered. "Sometimes, though, that don't seem so sure."

"Riddle me again," Long Tom suggested. "I like guessing games."

A thought struck Ace Jackson with all the visible effect

of a physical blow. He reared up on the hospital cot, heedless of the girl's admonishing gasp.

"Gimme straight dope on something," he requested.

"Sure," Long Tom said.

"Did Doc Savage send you to Santa Amoza?" Ace Jackson asked pointedly.

Long Tom's answer was prompt.

"I came here solely to see an old pal, who had cracked up. And for no other reason," he said. "Now what is this ranting about an Inca in Gray? Is it a secret?"

Ace Jackson sat up rigidly on the cot.

"You won't believe this," he clipped. "But I'll give it to you, anyway."

"Go ahead," Long Tom invited. "I'm rather gullible."

"The Inca in Gray is responsible for this war!" Ace Jackson leaned back as if he had gotten something heavy off his chest.

Long Tom squinted at the bandaged aviator.

"I suppose this Inca in Gray is the nickname of some general of Delezon, the country Santa Amoza is fighting," Long Tom suggested.

"You don't get me right," Ace Jackson corrected. "The Inca in Gray is something—something horrible. No one knows whether he is from Delezon, or what."

Ace Jackson sat up on the cot again. He leveled a gauze-wrapped arm at Long Tom.

"I'll give you one example," he said. "At one time the Santa Amoza army apparently had Delezon licked. We had broken through their lines in a big drive, and were marching across the desert toward their capital. Then, one night, every officer of consequence in the expeditionary force died, mysteriously. It was the work of the Inca in Gray."

"Sounds to me like the work of an espionage agent," Long Tom corrected.

Ace Jackson shook his head. "This Inca in Gray has done horrible things; murder, butcherings, things deliberately calculated to stir our nation into a frenzy. Our enemy, Delezon, would hardly do that. General Fernanez Vigo, commanding the enemy force, is a straight shooter, even if he is hell on wheels in a fight."

Long Tom grunted. "I still say espionage."

"I'll give you another example," Ace Jackson said. "There was——"

Entrancing Señorita Anita Carcetas interrupted.

"Let me give you the example of Señor Ace Jackson," she said.

9

Ace Jackson scowled at his bandages. "I look like a swell example."

THE GIRL went on as if she had not been interrupted.
"Ace Jackson is commander of our Santa Amoza air force," she explained. "He learned that a fever was sweeping a certain mountain tribe of natives. Serum was needed to save them. Ace Jackson volunteered to fly this serum to the spot to save these people."

"Am I blushing," Ace Jackson muttered.

"The Inca in Gray tried to kill Ace Jackson," the girl finished. "Our enemy, General Vigo, would not have tried that. The fever epidemic is as much in his country as in ours."

Long Tom shook his head. "This doesn't sound reasonable."

"I know it," Ace Jackson growled.

"Just who is this Inca in Gray?" Long Tom demanded.

"Mystery," Ace Jackson retorted. "Nobody knows. He is just a name that you hear whispered."

Señorita Anita Carcetas looked at Long Tom, but spoke to Ace Jackson, saying, "Ace, you might tell Long Tom what we were talking about this morning."

Long Tom interposed: "How did this Inca in Gray get you, Ace?"

"You know I never go up without going over my plane," Ace Jackson said. "I did this time not ten minutes before taking off. But a wing came off just the same. My parachute had been tampered with. It split, but evidently not as much as they had hoped. I got broke up some."

Long Tom nodded. "Now, what is this thing you were talking about?"

Ace Jackson opened his mouth to speak, then closed it. A door of the room had opened. A male nurse, the same one who had guided Long Tom, entered, carrying a glass of milk and some food on a tray. The nurse seemed very weary, as if he had worked long and hard hours. Perhaps, that explained the small accident which now befell him. An accident innocent of itself, but one which was to have grisly consequences.

He stumbled. Milk and viands landed on Long Tom's coat.

"Thousand pardons, señor," the nurse gasped contritely, seizing a towel and mopping at the mess he had made. The towel did not help much.

"Forget it," Long Tom said.

10

"No, no, señor, I will clean it," the male nurse gasped. "Only a few moments will be required."

Long Tom grinned and removed his coat.

"Sure, sure," he smiled, "if it'll make you happy."

The nurse took the coat, still bubbling over with apologies —possibly the presence of the president's daughter had helped unnerve him—and, backing to the door, used one hand behind him to open it. He stood there bowing again and again, half in the room and half out.

No one noticed that the arm over which he had draped Long Tom's coat was extended into the corridor while the rest of his person was in the hospital room.

"I am so sorry, señor," he told Long Tom again.

"Forget it," Long Tom repeated. "Accidents happen."

The nurse backed into the corridor and shut the door.

Señorita Anita Carcetas said: "Poor fellow, he is doubtless overworked."

Long Tom asked Ace Jackson: "Now, what were you about to tell——"

A sound came from the corridor outside the door, an unpleasant sound, obviously a body falling. And there was one shriek, brief but hideous, in a man's voice.

Long Tom swung to the door and wrenched it open. Señorita Anita Carcetas made a shrill sound, expressive of utter horror. Ace Jackson got out of his cot, could not stand, and slumped to the floor.

Long Tom looked up and down the corridor. No one was in sight. Then the electrical wizard bent over the body of the man on the hallway floor.

The man on the floor was on his back, dead, with his eyes open and a terrible agony reflected in their still depths. It was the nurse. Long Tom's soiled coat was still draped over his arm.

But it was the dead man's face that held Long Tom's gaze. The face was gray, almost white. Long Tom looked more closely to ascertain what made the dead man's face gray.

What looked like gray dust coated the fellow's features.

Long Tom fanned with his hand close to the visage of the corpse and the gray stuff was stirred like dust in a little cloud.

"Get away from it!" Ace Jackson screamed.

Chapter 3

SUBSTITUTED MESSAGE

WITHOUT TURNING, Long Tom rapped: "Why not touch it?"

"That man was killed by the Inca in Gray!" Ace Jackson shouted.

Long Tom spun around. "What?"

"The gray dust," Ace Jackson snapped, "is always on his victims."

Señorita Anita Carcetas said: "The death was meant for you, Señor Long Tom."

"I know it," Long Tom growled. "Only the coat on his arm was visible when he stood in the door. The killer thought it was me with my coat over my arm."

The word exchange had taken but a moment. Long Tom whipped glances up and down the corridor. He decided the fleeing killer would have gone to the right toward the exit. Long Tom ran in that direction.

He reached the entrance and saw a uniformed military guard there, rifle alert. The fellow must have heard the death sound.

"Did any one pass?" Long Tom demanded in Spanish. The sentry said no one had passed and Long Tom turned back, trying doors to the right and to the left. There were cries, running footsteps from other parts of the hospital, these no doubt made by persons coming to see what the excitement was about.

It was in a big white operating room, banked with instruments, that Long Tom came upon an object of interest.

The object was a man; a rather small man who was attired in immaculate blue serge. He had Latin handsomeness and a mustache that was a dark neat line on his upper lip.

There was a distinct smear of gray dust on the right sleeve of his blue serge suit.

Long Tom rushed to the small man's side. The fellow was struggling to get up, his writhing lips bending and unbending his black line of a mustache.

"A fiend—cloaked, masked," he gulped. "He struck me down and fled."

He pointed to an open window.

12

Long Tom whipped to the window. There was no one in sight. The ground below was sun baked enough not to hold footprints, and there was shrubbery enough about to have concealed a small army.

Long Tom shouted an alarm and a soldier appeared, began searching the grounds.

Going back to the neat little man with the mustache, Long Tom studied the fellow narrowly. Abruptly, Long Tom seized the man's arm.

"Free me!" the other sputtered. "What is the meaning?"

"You were attacked," Long Tom told him dryly. "But that's your story. You haven't got a mark on you."

The man tried to speak. But Long Tom shook him, then marched him, angrily incoherent, back to the room where Ace Jackson had gotten back on his cot.

Ace Jackson's eyes flew wide and he said: "Don't mind who you manhandle, do you?"

"What do you mean?" Long Tom growled.

Ace Jackson pointed at the mustached prisoner. "No idea who this is?"

"I don't get you," Long Tom said.

"He is Señor Junio Serrato," Ace Jackson advised.

"For the love of mud," said Long Tom.

"Exactly," Ace Jackson agreed. "Señor Serrato is war minister of this nation!"

Long Tom hurriedly released his captive. One did not drag war ministers around as if they were common culprits. For, in these South American countries, war ministers usually had more actual power than the president.

"I deeply regret my tremendous error, Señor Serrato," Long Tom murmured.

That was diplomacy. Regardless of what one thought, one did not accuse war ministers of crimes which there might be difficulty in proving they had committed.

Long Tom was somewhat surprised when Señor Junio Serrato took it graciously.

"It is no indignity to be handled roughly by a man who belongs to one of the most famous little groups in the world," he murmured. "I have heard much of Doc Savage and his five aides."

Long Tom was trying to think of something equally polite when there was an uproar out on the hospital grounds. They hurried to the windows and saw the squad of soldiers who had been searching the ground had made two seizures. They were bringing the prisoners in.

13

The captives were a Jeff and Mutt pair in stature. Both were well dressed.

"The *soldados* have made a mistake," war minister Serrato murmured at Long Tom's elbow.

"You know the prisoners?" Long Tom queried.

"Oh, yes," minister Serrato nodded.

"Count Hoffe is the tall one," minister Serrato explained. "He is the representative of the European munitions concern which supplies our needs in arms and ammunitions."

"The short one?" Long Tom suggested.

"Don Kurrell is his name," advised minister Serrato.

"Another munitions salesman?"

"Oh, no." The war minister smiled again. "Don Kurrell represents the company which holds the Santa Amoza oil concessions. He is interested in seeing the war ended. His oil wells, I regret to say, are in the battle zone. Unless our nation wins, his concern stands to lose its investment."

The prisoners were ushered in shortly. The soldiers explained they had been acting suspiciously when caught.

Tall Count Hoffe removed his hat, displaying a close-cropped bullet head, and explained: "We were seeking shelter. We heard the excitement and feared there might be shooting."

"Just why were you here?" Long Tom asked them.

The two looked at each other, then eyed minister Serrato, and they all glanced at Ace Jackson.

Ace Jackson said: "I think everybody has the same idea."

"What is it?" Long Tom demanded.

"The thing I started to tell you," Ace Jackson grunted.

"Shoot," Long Tom invited.

"We want Doc Savage down here," Ace Jackson said. "We want him to smash this devil, the Inca in Gray."

THERE WAS talk after that, explanations of what was known of the Inca in Gray. But all of it added up to little more than Long Tom had already heard. The Inca in Gray was some mysterious power who was managing to keep the slaughter going for some unknown reason of his own.

"I'll see about it," Long Tom told them finally. "I'll cable Doc," and left.

Hardly more than one minute after Long Tom had taken his departure, Count Hoffe clicked his heels, doubled his long body in a smart bow and said: "Believe me, I am truly glad that Doc may come to Santa Amoza. This unending slaughter is a terrible thing."

Then he took his departure.

Ace Jackson stared at the door after Count Hoffe had

14

gone, and closed it. He muttered, "Sometimes I wonder about that guy. He's the only one I can think of who stands to profit by having this war go on and on."

"You mean that he might be the Inca in Gray?" murmured war minister Serrato. "That thought has occurred to me."

"And to me, too," broke in Don Kurrell. "That is why I have been palling up with the blighter. I am checking up on him."

"Learn anything?" asked Ace Jackson.

"No," said Don Kurrell.

Every one left.

Those in the room would have been greatly interested in the actions of a strange figure in a nearby park some moments later. Even a close inspection would not show whether this form was that of man or woman.

An all-enveloping cloak of gray material, with a hood which completely concealed the features, furnished an excellent disguise. This form glided through the shrubbery, keeping out of sight, and stopped under a tree which grew out of the shrubbery. This tree was very large and ancient.

The actions of the mysterious skulker became rather unusual. The figure sank beside the tree, took out a notebook from beneath the cloak, and wrote something in it. The notebook had pages of thin, onionskin paper.

The note was rolled, and one hand, gloved, carried it into a hollow in the bottom of the tree. If the strange individual had made any sound thus far, it was lost in the cooing of pigeons, numbers of which swarmed the ancient park at all hours of the day, picking up scraps, perching in the branches of the trees.

The individual in gray removed his hand from the tree, and slunk away, vanishing from view.

Only a few moments later, a pigeon arose from the top of the tree. It was only one pigeon among many, and there was nothing to indicate to any onlooker that it was a carrier pigeon, which had come up from the hollow trunk of the old tree from a cote concealed in the base. Nor was there anything to show an observer on the ground that the bird carried a note sealed in a quill.

LONG TOM ROBERTS was also encountering pigeons, but they were only of the ordinary mongrel variety which hopped about in the streets and he paid no attention to them. Long Tom was thinking, mulling over in his mind what he was convinced was a fact, two facts rather.

The two facts were the two attempts on his life—the

attempt of the beggar horde, and the strange incident at the hospital. Presumably, both attempts had been made by the Inca in Gray; and the motive was not hard to guess. Doc Savage was not wanted on the Santa Amoza scene.

This talk of the Inca in Gray was entirely new to Long Tom. But that was not strange. This war between Santa Amoza and Delezon had been going its bloody way for almost four years, yet it was quite possible that any number of people in New York had never heard of it. The newspapers, of course, had carried stories of the bigger battles, but almost nothing of the day-by-day fight. American editorials usually dismissed the affairs as sporadic squabbles over the jungle and desert tract that separated the two republics. Washington had, however, placed an embargo on the export of arms to the belligerents, hoping to stop the conflict.

"I'll bet Count Hoffe liked that," Long Tom muttered.

The electrical wizard turned into a cable office. He took a blank and wrote:

DOC SAVAGE
  NEW YORK
  EVENT VERY MYSTERIOUS STOP LEARN WAR BEING KEPT GOING BY MYSTERY INDIVIDUAL KNOWN AS INCA IN GRAY STOP MIGHT BE GOOD IDEA IF YOU CAME DOWN AND CLEANED UP
                              LONG TOM

Long Tom left the cable office and blissfully went his way, searching for a suitable hotel.

Some moments after Long Tom had left, when there had been approximately time for him to get out of earshot, a strange thing happened. A man came running wildly down the street with several others pursuing him. He turned into the cable office as if he thought it offered escape. There he picked up a chair and turned, at bay. The pursuers charged in. Promptly there was a mêlée. Furniture flew about. Desks were upset. The cable office attendants screamed for the police.

The police arrived eventually. But, by that time, the mysterious fighters had taken their departure. They had, in fact, joined the sinister figure which had dispatched the pigeon from the park tree.

"How did it come out?" the cloaked individual asked.

"Perfectly, master," came the answer.

One of the gang who had staged the fight turned over a

16

telegraph blank. It was the one which bore the message Long Tom had written.

The hooded one chuckled when he saw this.

"You left in its place the one I gave you?" he asked.

"We did," said the other.

"It is well," the cloaked one said. "Had we merely stolen the message the cable attendants might have missed it."

"We did excellent work," bragged one of the fighters.

"True," said the cloaked one. "Your work is not done."

The other seemed surprised, and made a question with his eyebrows.

"Long Tom Roberts is now to be gotten out of the way," the cloaked one clipped shortly.

LONG TOM had finally found himself a hotel.

"My luggage get here, señor?" he demanded of the clerk.

The clerk smiled, all but bumped his forehead on the desk in a bow, and passed over Long Tom's room key.

Long Tom located the stairway and climbed to a hall which was dark after the brilliance of the sunlight outside. It took him a moment or two to locate the room that his key called for. He unlocked it and, his eyes still somewhat blinded, he swung the door open.

Two men had been busy over Long Tom's open suitcase. They leaped to their feet. Knives came into their hands with grim suddenness.

Long Tom was afraid of no man with a knife. Anyway, there was a chair between himself and the pair. He could grab it, use it for a weapon.

But he did not reach the chair. The two over the suitcase had been there as bait to hold his attention. There was another man standing just inside the door. That fellow went forward, swinging an arm club fashion. His hand held a gun, held it by the butt. For nobody but a fool clubs with the butt of a gun.

The two, who had been over the suitcase, caught the electrical wizard's unconscious form so that it would not make noise in falling.

A strange figure in a cloak now appeared, coming from somewhere outside. This individual examined Long Tom closely, making sure that he was senseless.

"Bring a trunk," the cloaked one ordered. "We are going to take him away."

"Is it safe, O Inca in Gray?" one asked.

"Keep your suggestions to yourselves," uttered their fantastic looking chief. "Get this Long Tom Roberts to the place at the edge of the city where I shall meet you."

17

Chapter 4

THE PERIL IN NEW YORK

IN THE QUIET pre-evening activity of New York, rather peculiar sounds could be heard. They were on the eighty-sixth floor of a building which was probably the most pretentious skyscraper in the city.

"*Oink!*" The sound came with distinct regularity. "*Oink! Oink!*"

Two men sat in the eighty-sixth floor office from which the sounds came. One of them looked angry. He was a rather slender man, especially thin at the waist. But the thing about him that stood out was his garments. They were sartorial perfection. A typical sample of what was gaining for the wearer a reputation as perhaps the nation's best dresser.

"*Oink!*" came the sound. "*Oink!*"

The second man in the room kept his face straight with some difficulty. This man looked rather pleasantly like an ape in unkempt civilized clothing. He would undoubtedly weigh in excess of two hundred and fifty pounds.

The apish man was making the sound, doing it systematically and with painstaking care.

"*Oink!*" he tried again. "*Oink! Oink!*"

The dapper man blew up. He gesticulated with a slender black cane which he had been holding across his knee.

"Monk," he gritted, "just one more of those noises and I'm going to trim your toenails off right next to your ears."

"Now, Ham," the apish Monk murmured, "you should control that temper."

Ham got up and did something with his cane so that it became evident that harbored therein was a blade of fine steel which looked razor sharp.

"You've been making those hog noises to devil me," he said grimly. "You are hunting trouble and you are certainly going to get accommodated."

Neither of these men looked quite what he was. The man with sartorially perfect raiment, "Ham," was Brigadier General Theodore Marley Brooks, pride of the Harvard Law School alumni. The simian one, "Monk," was Lieutenant Colonel Andrew Blodgett Mayfair, admittedly one of the greatest industrial chemists.

These two—like Long Tom of the South American happenings—were members of Doc Savage's group of five aides. The spot where they conducted their quarrel was the anteroom of Doc Savage's headquarters.

Monk squared off belligerently and picked up a chair as a defense against the sword cane, but before anything happened, a voice spoke from the doorway.

"Something seems to have happened to Long Tom in South America," the voice said.

THAT VOICE was remarkable, not that it was loud or that it seemed to strive to be particularly emphatic. But it had a suppressed quality that induced thoughts of a mighty machine, murmuring under low throttle.

Monk and Ham both whirled to stare at Doc Savage as he came into the room.

Doc Savage held a cablegram in one hand. The hand was distinctive for two things. The tendons on the back were amazing. The hand had an unusual bronze color. The size of the hand was mentionable also, but was not especially striking because the rest of the man's size was in proportion.

An individual whose appearance was in keeping with his fabulous reputation was this man, Doc Savage. He would stand out in a multitude. There was more to it than his appearance. His eyes for instance—they were like pools of flake gold, stirred always by tiny winds. And there was also his hair, the hue a slightly darker bronze than his skin and straight, rather remarkably like a metallic skullcap.

Doc Savage offered the cablegram. Monk and Ham read it.

DOC SAVAGE
   NEW YORK
   IN ALCALA SANTA AMOZA VISITING FRIEND ACE JACKSON STOP MAY SPEND SOME TIME HERE STOP EVERYTHING QUIET

                                    LONG TOM

The cablegram had come from Alcala, Santa Amoza.

Monk, the homely chemist, squinted and scratched his bullet head.

"I don't see anything in that to make anybody think Long Tom is in trouble," he said.

"For once I agree with the ape here," Ham murmured. "I don't either."

Doc Savage's metallic features did not change expression. This was one of his characteristics. He rarely showed emotion.

"Have you overlooked the five-letter code?" he asked.

19

Monk started, and a ludicrous expression crossed his homely face.

"Sure," he grunted, "every sentence should start with a five-letter word. That's the touch to make sure members of our gang really send the messages."

Dapper Ham seized the cablegram which Doc had brought and examined it again.

"Every sentence doesn't start with a five-letter word in this," he snapped. "That means Long Tom did not send it."

Monk scratched in the bristles along his nape. "What do you reckon's behind this?"

"We will see what we can learn by cabling," Doc told him.

On the street there was not much traffic and not many parked cars. Hence, there was plenty of room along the curbing. A small sedan wheeled into one of these open spaces.

Four men alighted. The fifth, who was behind the wheel, drove the car away. Those who had gotten out strolled over and ostensibly looked into a show-window. Above them towered the stone and steel monolith that housed Doc Savage's eighty-sixth floor aerie.

"Your instructions are clearly understood?" asked one of the men.

The others nodded.

The leader paced the way into the skyscraper. He was a rather striking fellow, principally because of his size and shape. His lines were somewhat remindful of a box on stiff legs. He looked as hard as railroad ties.

Under one arm this man carried a bulky object, carefully wrapped in thick brown paper.

Once in the building lobby, the men separated. Two turned toward the elevator that would lead them to an observation tower above Doc Savage's headquarters, almost a hundred stories above the street level.

The other two members of the group strolled carelessly down the spacious lobby, stopping close to the entrance that led to the express elevator which carried passengers to floors eighty to ninety. They lighted cigarettes and leaned idly against the wall, conversing softly as if awaiting the appearance of friends.

Over in the observation tower elevator, the box of a man—he had the unmistakable look of a professional wrestler—and his companion were silent. The operator glanced at them with only slight curiosity, for dwellers in Manhattan become accustomed to strange types of humanity.

When the elevator stopped at the observation floor, the

20

two passengers acquired admission tickets, walked out on the railed platform and gawked about. A few other persons were there, these obviously being tourists. The burly wrestler still carried his package as he mingled with the crowd. There was system in the mingling, however, for the pair worked around the tower and soon stood before a small door. They tried this and found it locked.

They waited until they were alone on that side of the tower. Then the wrestler brought out a bunch of keys—an assortment of skeleton keys. There was a faint click and the door opened.

The pair slipped through and closed the door behind them. Without hesitation they raced down a small set of steps into a room where the whirr and the click of machinery sounded continuously.

It was the room which held the mechanism that operated the elevators.

A mechanic rose quickly from his chair just inside the room with the machinery. But he was too slow. He did not even see the newcomers. The wrestler swung a great block of a fist, and the mechanic was senseless.

"You know what we do next?" the big box of a man asked.

He was looking about, plainly more than a little bewildered by the maze of wheels and cables that confronted him.

His companion nodded, a confident grin on his wizened face.

"I can handle the rest of it," he said. "I used to install these things."

With sure steps he threaded his way through the cables, pointed to one drum which appeared full of slender steel thread.

"This is the cable that holds up Doc Savage's private elevator," he said. "Unlimber that thing you're carryin'."

The big man grunted and unwrapped the parcel which had been under his arm. The other took it, stripped off the wrapping and revealed a compact metal-cutting torch of a type popular with safe robbers.

Eye-hurting flame from the torch began to play against the cable drum.

Down in the street level lobby, the two men who were leaning against the wall near the express elevator were beginning to consult their watches nervously.

"We got another minute," one said.

They were silent throughout the minute.

21

"Now," the first said. And the other nodded.

They walked to the endmost of the bank of express elevators and entered the cage.

The operator spoke to them quietly, saying, "This elevator goes only to Doc Savage's floor."

"That's where we're headed," one of the passengers responded.

Then the operator jumped suddenly and looked down. A gun had been jammed into his ribs.

"Get going," the hard-faced holder of the gun ordered.

The operator closed the door and started up. For an instant, the two passengers were speechless, their eyes intent on the operator. The latter moved his lever to the stop position. The button of the apparatus that would automatically level the cage at the eighty-sixth floor door was already pushed in.

A fist struck the elevator man callously under the jaw. He sagged, and one of the two passengers caught him under the arms. Holding him helpless, they hit him again and again, until his senses were thoroughly beaten out.

They lowered him to the floor as the cage stopped on the eighty-sixth floor.

The two passengers opened the door, made sure the corridor was empty, then propped the elevator door open with the use of small wooden wedges, which they had previously prepared. They moved silently down the corridor to the stairway. One of them turned and cupped his hands to his mouth.

"Help!" he screamed. "Help!"

Then the pair scuttled silently down the stairway.

The door of Doc Savage's quarters burst open. The giant bronze man was first through, Monk and Ham close on his heels.

"Somebody yelled!" Monk exploded. "Where was it?"

The open elevator door caught their attention. They ripped toward it, glanced inside.

Unexpectedly a small weird sound filled the corridor and the elevator cage wherein the beaten unconscious operator lay. The sound was tiny, exotic, a thing difficult of description. It was a trilling, in a sense, a minute, fantastic note that might have been the product of the wind through the spires of an arctic ice field.

Monk and Ham looked at Doc Savage, knowing the bronze man was making the sound. They had heard it often. It was a small thing which the bronze man did unconsciously in moments of stress.

22

Doc Savage stepped into the elevator. Monk and Ham followed.

HIGH ABOVE, in the room which housed the lifting machinery, the two sinister men had been staring downward. The elevator cage had a grilled top and the interior was brightly lighted so that they saw Doc Savage and his two aides enter.

"Quick!' gulped the wrestler.

The other manipulated the cutting torch. He already used it sufficiently to nearly sever the cables. The finish of the job required only a moment. With the sound of a snapping fiddle string, the cable parted.

The cage fell away from the open door before Doc Savage and his aides could possibly get out. It gathered momentum. Doc worked the elevator control lever rapidly. It had no effect. Their speed increased.

Homely Monk jammed a thumb violently against the button which was labeled emergency stop. Nothing happened. His apish visage began to look as if whitewash were being pumped under the skin.

Floors went past in a grisly blur.

"Cable cut," Doc Savage said briefly. "Automatic stopping device jammed."

Ham, the dapper lawyer, said nothing, but brushed an imaginary speck of dust from his immaculate clothing as if he wanted to look his best when his crushed body was found after the elevator crashed to the bottom of the shaft, eighty-six floors below.

Doc Savage's bronze features had not lightened. The paleness of fear, which might have been expected, was entirely absent. His features were almost weirdly composed. Nor did he speak.

Air was roaring about the cage as they plummeted. The senseless operator stirred a little on the floor, but he would never revive in time to realize what was happening.

The wild cage flashed past the ground floor. And a startled yell came from the starter outside as he realized what was occurring.

Things happened. A giant hand seemed to reach out and grab the elevator, gently at first, then with more violence. Air, passing the sides of the cage, made an ear-splitting scream. The occupants of the elevator went down as if mashed by a giant invisible hand.

And the cage was unexpectedly still, although it seemed, due to the freakishness of the human organism, that it was now flying upward.

23

Monk lay very still. Ham had fallen half across him.

They both eyed Doc Savage. Their expressions showed what they wanted—explanations.

"The bottoms of these shafts are of special construction," Doc Savage said. "They are completely enclosed and fit tightly to the sides of the cage. The compression of the air formed a natural shock absorber."

Monk started to say something, then looked down at his clothing, surprised. He had become soaking wet with nervous perspiration.

ESCAPE FROM the cage did not prove to be a simple matter. First, the top grille was bolted in place solidly and, being stout, it yielded but slowly. Springing upward, Doc Savage managed to seize an ornamental projection in the cage top. An observer would have sworn it offered no hand grip whatever. Yet, the bronze giant clung there and struck and wrenched repeatedly at the grating until it came loose. The metal was a stout alloy. He bent it back amid a squeaking and rending.

By this time, they had the shaft door open and faces were shoved through, shouting excitedly that an emergency truck had been summoned.

The sides of the shaft were of brick, and rough. Doc Savage mounted, the strength in his amazing hands making ample security out of microscopic handholds.

Even with his efforts, however, several minutes had elapsed before he reached the lobby. A crowd milled. More persons came in from the street, excitement drawn.

Doc Savage lost no time in getting the doors closed so that no one might enter or leave. There was a bare chance the culprits might be inside.

They were not. They had lost no time in leaving the skyscraper, had entered their little sedan and were driving fast when they got a glimpse of the bronze man.

The big wrestler and his consorts were not bad actors. They managed not to show enough excitement to attract attention.

"We've laid an egg," one muttered.

The wrestler began to curse, calling his own father and mother and immediate ancestors numerous unpleasant names.

"Count Hoffe in South America ain't gonna like this," another of them groaned.

The wrestler stopped abusing his ancestors.

"We sure gave the job a botching," he agreed. "Now Doc Savage will stem straight for South America."

24

"And the Inca in Gray will begin to lay eggs of his own," another man agreed.

"Don't worry," snorted the wrestler. "Any eggs the Inca in Gray lays will hatch out plenty of hell."

The little sedan took them out of sight.

An hour later, Doc Savage knew that those who attempted to murder them had escaped. The bronze man went to his laboratory. He began assembling mechanical devices —the gadgets which he employed and which, on more than one occasion, had saved his life.

Monk, the homely chemist, stopped in the reception room to read a newspaper. Doc Savage interrupted Monk's perusal of the newspaper.

"You might get your portable laboratory together, Monk," he suggested.

The homely chemist squinted at the bronze giant. "Then we're going places?"

"We are," Doc agreed.

Monk frowned. "Do you think that fake cable with Long Tom's name signed to it, and that attempt to kill us had a connection?"

Whatever reply Doc Savage intended to make was interrupted by the appearance of a messenger, wearing the uniform of a cable company. He presented a blue envelope, which Doc opened, read, then passed to Monk and Ham. The missive was cryptic, expressive.

DOC SAVAGE
   NEW YORK
    LONG TOM ROBERTS HAS DISAPPEARED
                          ACE JACKSON

The message was from Alcala, Santa Amoza.

Monk looked up from the missive and demanded: "This means we charge right down there, don't it?"

"It does," Doc agreed.

Ham asked, "Do we go by plane?"

"We will try the new stratosphere dirigible," Doc told him. "On a flight as long as this, it will probably be faster than our big plane."

Chapter 5

FIRING SQUAD

AT ABOUT that moment, Long Tom Roberts, some thousands of miles south of New York, lay on his back and wished that Doc Savage were not quite so far distant. He also wondered where he was, what had been done to him.

He got around to trying to move and found his arms and legs tied. A bit later, it dawned on him that he was jammed in a cramped compartment, small for his scrawny frame. He tried to shift his position a little.

Instantly, ripping swear words in *Español* crackled above him. He was kicked twice, very hard, in the side. Then a pair of heavy, booted feet pressed down on his middle and remained there, effectually discouraging further movement on his part.

Long Tom lay still and organized his thoughts. He was in a plane, an open cockpit type ship.

A riveting machine seemed to open up, almost over his head. The terrific din of it made such a pain in Long Tom's head that he gasped and shut his eyes tightly. The plane in which he was riding must be engaged in a fight.

There was a sound not unlike two cats having a violent fight in the rear of the fuselage somewhere. The plane's framework trembled perceptibly. Long Tom had been through enough aerial fighting to know what the sound meant. Machine gun bullets hitting their ship.

Long Tom's ears began to distinguish other sounds, which resembled firecrackers letting go in a well. That would be artillery. There was an occasional much closer *woof!* some of which cause the plane to sway, pitch. Archies.

Long Tom lay back and shut his eyes. He was not scared, not by the war anyway. He had been through too many of those. He did some reflecting.

Let's see. He had been knocked out in the Alcala hotel. Now he had awakened over the front lines of a war which, judging from the sounds, was no opera.

Long Tom, who frequently went out of his way to hunt trouble, seemed to have done very well in the present case.

The war front sounds were dropping behind. There was no more machine gunning, no more anti-aircraft. The plane flew quietly for some time.

Then arms caught Long Tom under the shoulder, yanked him up. Sunlight hit him in the eyes so blindingly that he was hardly able to see. He felt the ropes being ripped from his feet. A knife slashed the cords that bound his arms.

Instantly, Long Tom turned, tried to get a grip on his captor; but the confinement had made the pallid electrical expert very clumsy. He fared very badly in the fight which he started.

Powerful arms caught him about the middle, lifted him up. He was held over the side of the cockpit, the whole thing happening so quickly that he was distinctly astonished to find himself plunging like a rock toward a mass of very green jungle some thousands of feet below!

LONG TOM'S next actions were pure instinct. He reached for a parachute rip cord ring. When he did that, truth was, he did not even know whether he wore a chute. The head blows had left him very hazy. But the chute rip cord ring was there. He yanked it.

With a suddenness that wrenched his aching muscles, his downward plunge was halted by a billowing spread of silk that snapped out over his head. The parachute had opened, checking his fall.

Long Tom, however, failed to experience the feeling of relief which this happening should have induced. The shock of parachute opening had been too much for his shaky condition. It had knocked him out. He hung, quite senseless, in the parachute harness.

Long Tom, being unconscious, missed the excitement which his descent caused. The jungle land below was not far behind the front lines, and it was infested correspondingly by soldiers.

Naturally, no one shot at the figure in the parachute; but there was a wild rush for the spot where the silk lobe was going to drop.

Long Tom hit hard, but did not know it. He was also dragged a few yards until the silken bulb of the parachute caught itself on a small tree and spilled its air.

When Long Tom revived a few seconds later, he was out of the parachute harness and being held erect by several men. There were other men standing about, holding rifles. All of the men wore uniforms.

Suddenly Long Tom peered at the uniforms more closely. They were not like the uniforms he had seen in Alcala. They were entirely different, in fact. He realized what the difference meant.

"Blazes!" Long Tom gulped feebly.

He must be across the line in Santa Amoza's enemy country, Delezon.

The soldiers who had seized him were looking him over. The officer in charge wore a design on his sleeve which meant, if Long Tom guessed correctly, that he was a corporal.

"*Norte Americano*," said the corporal.

"*Si, si*," Long Tom said in Spanish. "I'm an American. Where am I?"

The corporal laughed; it was not a nice laugh.

"Search him," directed the corporal.

The soldiers plunged hands into his pockets, turning them inside out, bringing to light everything in his possesson. The possessions were a distinct surprise to Long Tom. He was, he discovered, carrying things he had never seen before.

There was, for instance, a small bottle with a poison label. There was a tiny camera with a very fast lens. There was a fountain pen which held, as the corporal in charge of the soldiers demonstrated, invisible ink.

"Boy, oh boy," Long Tom mumbled thickly. "Somebody has sure done carpenter work on me."

"What you ees mean, señor?" asked the corporal, who seemed to understand a little English.

"I've been framed," Long Tom said.

The corporal emitted another loud laugh, even more ugly, if that were possible, than the first one.

"Eet ees plain you are spy, señor," he said.

"I've been framed," Long Tom repeated.

"You need more better story than that," said the corporal. "Mebbe yo ees t'ink of better one as we take yo to thees Señor General Fernanez Vigo."

"General Vigo, dictator general of Delezon?" Long Tom grunted.

"*Si, si, señor*," agreed the corporal. "General Vigo, he ees like talk to spy."

GENERAL FERNANEZ VIGO proved to be in a dugout rather closer to the thundery, crashing front line trenches than a general might be expected to keep himself.

General Vigo was the biggest and ugliest man Long Tom could recall having seen in a long time. General Vigo's inconspicuous khaki garb only accentuated his gargantuan aspect. No chevrons or insignia showed on his uniform. As a matter of fact, Long Tom reflected, such marks of rank would not be needed. For any one who had ever heard of General Vigo would recognize him on sight.

General Vigo's laugh was also interesting. It sounded as if a turkey gobbler were gobbling.

The gobble was very loud and very amused as General Vigo listened to Long Tom's attempt to explain that the spy paraphernalia found in his pockets had been planted there without his knowledge, and that he had not jumped from the plane but had been thrown.

Long Tom gave it up, not having expected the story to be believed anyway, and fell to eying General Vigo. He had heard of dictators, political iron men, and had seen some. This was the first one who had looked the part.

General Vigo stopped his gobble and rumbled in surprisingly good English, "You are a spy. You are wasting your time to deny it."

Long Tom frowned at the world's ugliest man. "What happens to spies over here?"

"They are shot," General Vigo boomed promptly.

"Do they get a chance to defend themselves?" the electrical wizard countered.

"That depends on me," General Vigo laughed. "Sometimes, yes, if I get up on what you call the right side of the bed. Otherwise, no. We just go ahead and shoot them."

"How soon do you shoot them?" Long Tom asked.

General Vigo shrugged. "In your case, ten minutes."

Long Tom batted both eyes rapidly. He was quite positive General Vigo was not kidding him. The General looked very serious at the moment. Long Tom moistened his lips.

"Can you get a cablegram to New York?" he asked.

"*Si, si,*" said General Vigo in answer, and added, "Sure."

"Take a tip," Long Tom suggested. "Cable Doc Savage before you cut loose on me."

General Vigo looked like a man who has just discovered himself standing over a quicksand bed.

"Doc Savage?" he growled. "What do you mean, señor?"

"Ask Doc Savage to describe his aide Long Tom Roberts to you," Long Tom suggested. "Take a good look at me when you get the description."

General Vigo thought that over. That he had heard of Doc Savage, it was plain.

"You are one of Doc Savage's men?" General Vigo demanded.

"Right," Long Tom told him.

"What do you do down here, señor?"

Long Tom told him, making the recital as complete as he possibly could. He began with the moment when news of Ace Jackson's being in an Alcala hospital had come to him on the hydro-electric project far to the south.

Long Tom finished his recital, "And I have a hunch this mysterious power they call the Inca in Gray is behind my troubles."

General Vigo's face froze. For perhaps a score of seconds, he gave an excellent imitation of a man who had turned suddenly to stone. Then he turned slowly to Long Tom.

"Inca in Gray?" he said slowly and distinctly.

"Yes," said Long Tom. "Inca in Gray——"

"What do you know of the Inca in Gray?" General Vigo roared unexpectedly.

"Nothing," gulped Long Tom, startled. "You see I——"

General Vigo leaped to the mouth of the dugout, shouted, waved his arms. Soldiers came running. He bellowed orders at them in Spanish.

"This man has been found to be a spy!" he roared. "Take him to headquarters! He will be shot at once!"

LONG TOM had often boasted that he had a poker face, but it did not function very well now. He was already very low physically. His feelings showed on his face. The result was rather hideous.

Long Tom was taken well behind the lines, and was loaded into a motor van. This bumped and jarred and rumbled over a bad road, and probably no road at all, for a long time.

Because bouncing about on the van bottom was extremely uncomfortable, Long Tom managed to get to his feet, and this gave him a vantage point from which he could look out of the rear of the van. His impression that the truck was traversing what amounted to no road at all was correct. Scrawny jungle was reeling past. The van stirred up a great deal of evil looking gray dust. Long Tom almost shivered. The dust looked exactly like the dust of death which had been on the murdered man in the Alcala hospital.

Thatched huts began to appear on either side of the van. They were entering a village. The thatched huts gave way to mud or adobe structures. Then there was a scattering of stone buildings.

The van stopped. Long Tom was booted out. The soldiers were not handling him any too gently.

A figure appeared before them—the ugliest man in the world, again. To arrive so soon, General Vigo must have come ahead of them in a fast car.

Rage stiffened Long Tom's frail-looking frame. He made a jaw at General Vigo.

"You're putting your neck out, you old bull-head," Long Tom advised him.

30

"What does that mean—putting my neck out?" General Vigo demanded.

"It means likely a head chopping," Long Tom assured him. "In other words you're asking for it."

"Hah!" General Vigo struck an attitude, his idea of the one which Napoleon is generally supposed to have originated. He gobbled a laugh.

"Me, you would threaten?" he rumbled. "Me, General Vigo, you would scare? Hah! I am not afraid. Me, I can whip the world!"

"You been trying to whip Santa Amoza for four years," Long Tom said dryly.

Long Tom fully expected that to throw General Vigo into a rage. It did nothing of the sort, made General Vigo grin from ear to ear.

"A wise señor, eh," chuckled the dictator of Delezon. "I could like you. It is too bad I must shoot you."

Long Tom growled, "If you will get in touch with Doc Savage——"

General Vigo roared at his soldiers and waved an arm. The uniformed men picked Long Tom up, stalked with him toward a high adobe wall.

THE PROSPECTIVE shooting of a spy is a spectacle calculated to grip the attention of every one in the vicinity. This probably accounted for the fact of no one noticing the peculiar actions of one man observing the tableau.

This observer was not much to look at. He had a pocked face, was undersized, but, somehow, there was an air of evil about him. He was careful to get in no one's way and attract no attention, but this man kept a very close watch on what was happening to Long Tom.

General Vigo led the execution squad with the victim directly to the adobe stockade. This was very high and the walls seemed to be thick. There were embrasures to permit the mounting of machine guns along the top. It was obviously a fort.

The entrance through the wall was narrow, to make defense easier, and the aperture was closed by a door of heavy timbers. This opened. Long Tom was shoved through.

The stockade interior was occupied by numerous large buildings, most of them with barred windows. Long Tom was not given much time to look around. They hauled him across the court and he found himself standing before a wall.

The electrical wizard twisted his head to get a look at the wall. What he saw caused him to swallow. The wall was full of pits which had been made, no doubt, by rifle bullets. So here was where they shot their spies.

"A blindfold?" General Vigo inquired, much too politely.

"Yes," Long Tom said promptly.

General Vigo seemed surprised, but before he could speak, Long Tom explained.

"I don't want to be looking at the fellow who kills me," he said. "He might have bad dreams."

Contrarily enough, that struck General Vigo as extremely funny. His roar of laughter echoed off the walls, and sounded exactly like the noise of a farmyard turkey.

"Ready!" he bawled at the execution squad.

That shouted word was very loud. It carried beyond the compound wall and reached the ears of the crowd which had gathered outside. These curious persons had not been admitted to the stockade. Apparently no spectators were allowed. A tense silence settled over this small throng.

"Aim!" They all heard General Vigo shout the word.

If anything, the tension, the silence, increased.

On the outskirts of the listening crowd stood the insignificant man with the pocked face, the fellow who had been observing the proceedings with such interest. He strained his ears.

"Fire!" came General Vigo's command.

It was almost drowned by a volley of rifle shots. In the midst of the ragged fusillade, every one in the listening throng distinctly heard a cry of agony, exactly such a scream as a man would utter when he feels death lead in his vitals.

Silence followed that.

STRANGELY ENOUGH, only one man in the throng outside the stockade smiled. Every one else was sober. Death was not a pleasant thing.

But one man smiled, and that man was the pock-faced, curious spectator. After permitting himself the smile, he turned and scuttled back among the huts. He lost himself in the shabbier part of the village.

In one respect this village resembled the capital city of Santa Amoza, Alcala. It had stray pigeons. There was not a great number of them, but, nevertheless, there were pigeons.

So no one noted one particular pigeon which arose shortly from the village and winged in the direction of Santa Amoza. Certainly, no one caught the significance of the bird, because carrier pigeons look very much like ordinary pigeons.

Long Tom Roberts was dead. The bird carried word of the end of Doc Savage's aide.

Chapter 6

ATTACK IN THE AIR

THE AIR SPEED indicator needle stood near three-hundred-miles-an-hour; but the instrument was not entirely reliable. Not that it was defective—up here in the stratosphere there were wind currents, terrific in velocity, which carried an aircraft hither and yon so that only by celestial observation could speed be reliably calculated.

Doc Savage, a giant of bronze, leaned over a lighted map board, marking their position.

"At this speed, we should be in Alcala, capital of Santa Amoza, in another three hours," he said quietly.

Monk, a grotesque, baboon figure in the vague light of the stratosphere airship control cabin, lifted a furry hand to stifle a yawn.

"This chariot sure can travel," he muttered sleepily.

No clouds were about them, for they were too high. A cotton mass of vapor was some thousands of feet below. It was night. The clouds underneath had the aspect of silver which needed polishing in spots. Overhead the sky looked remarkably black, the stars unnaturally bright.

Ham, dapperly clad as usual, was in the rear of the control room, applying a bilious looking substance to the tip of his sword cane. The bilious concoction was a drugged mixture which would produce abrupt unconsciousness should a victim be pricked. Ham finished his task and came forward.

He said, "Doc, if you wish to get some sleep, Monk and myself can handle the craft."

Doc Savage shook his head. "Not tired. You and Monk turn in."

Ham nodded agreement, turned, and immediately stumbled over something that emitted a startled grunt.

Monk's bulky form straightened, his homely face contorted with what, if it was not rage, was an excellent imitation.

"Be careful, you fashion plate!" Monk howled. "You kicked that hog on purpose."

Ham sniffed and managed to do it with great dignity.

"Get your insect out of the way," he requested.

The homely Monk, registering great indignation, began to examine the object over which Ham had stumbled. This was a pig. The shote was one of striking appearance, having

33

a scrawny body, the legs of a dog, an inquiring snout, and ears which induced thoughts of a young elephant.

The pig was Habeas Corpus, Monk's pet.

Monk picked Habeas up by one over-sized ear, looked him over, and sat him down again, then glared at Ham. The dapper lawyer glared back. They did this as a matter of habit. Not only did they never speak civilly to each other, but they invariably looked as if they were on the point of indulging in mutual murder.

Doc Savage had resumed his position calculations. The speed of the dirigible and more especially the velocity and vagary of the air currents made frequent checks necessary. The lighter-than-air craft was much more subject to being swept off its course than would have been a heavier plane.

ALL SEEMED peaceful, safe, aboard the unusual aircraft. But appearances are deceptive.

Dirigibles are, of necessity, complicated craft, with many structural intricacies. In this one, for instance, there was a little tunnel of a catwalk running underneath from bow to stern, and another on top. There were various chimneylike tunnels with ladders. It was possible to reach almost any part of the gas bag by this system of passages. They were there so that repairs might be made easily while in the air.

They furnished an excellent hiding place; and, as such, they had been taken advantage of.

Two men crouched in one of the tunnels. Both of them had been with the gang which attempted to murder Doc Savage with the elevator trap in New York City. One was the burly fellow whose physical build somewhat resembled that of a box with short legs.

It was very cold up here in the stratosphere. The two skulkers, stowaways in fact, were blue, and almost too stiff to shiver. They had to hold hands over their mouths so that breath could warm their blue lips, in fact, before they could whisper to each other. They had been doing this for the last few moments, preparatory to a conversation.

"We can't hold out much longer," whispered the box-of-a-man's companion.

The burly fellow tried to agree with a nod, but was so cold he could hardly manage even that slight motion. "We're gonna freeze stiff," he said.

"This is a helluva hiding place," the other complained.

"We was damn lucky to get away with even this," the burly fellow told his companion earnestly.

"This Doc Savage ain't such hot stuff," said the first. "He didn't find out we were aboard."

The other man now managed a pronounced shiver which was not due entirely to the cold.

"Don't fool yourself," he mumbled. "The bronze guy took off in a heck of a hurry for South America."

They were silent for a time, suffering from the chills. Moving their arms and legs did them little good. They had not stowed away entirely unprepared, it might have been noted. Each had a small rubber bag, which was one of the chemical heating pads frequently sold by drugstores. That these were losing their potency was evident.

"We gotta do somethin'," said the small man.

The box of a fellow nodded. He crawled to one side, taking great care to avoid noise, and peered down through a tiny opening which he had made in the dirigible's skin. He joined his companion hurriedly.

"Looks like Santa Amoza below," he grunted. "It's time we opened our keg of nails."

The small man got up hurriedly. His expression was vicious, bloodthirsty, and just a bit uneasy.

"You think this is gonna work?" he grunted.

"Sure," said the other. "It can't fail."

They crept downward.

Doc Savage, plotting a Sumner line in the course of his navigation calculations, abruptly heard a slight sound. He heard it twice before giving it much attention. The noise was metallic, not a clanking, but a grinding and gritting, such as might have been made by pliers working upon metal.

Doc Savage swung a glance at the instrument panel. The dirigible was being guided by a robot pilot, a gyroscopic affair, not greatly different from those employed in big planes. The dirigible was exactly on its course.

Doc Savage abruptly decided Monk and Ham were not making the noise. Monk and Ham, in fact, were probably asleep.

The bronze man left the control room, went down a passage which was narrow, barely wide enough to permit him to pass, in fact.

Doc Savage reached the compartment which Monk and Ham used for sleeping. There were two of these, one on either side of the central passage.

The bronze man at once noted a strange fact. There were fastenings on the outside of the compartment doors. These were now secured. Monk and Ham, it appeared, were each locked in. Whether they were asleep could not be told. It was by no means silent enough for snores to be heard.

Doc Savage was looking at the barred doors when another

35

door directly ahead of him opened. This door led into the after catwalk which ran up to the tail where the rudders and elevators were affixed.

A small man with a pinched face that would have been an excellent visage for a movie villain, stepped out. He held his hands up, empty. He looked scared, in fear of receiving immediate bodily damage.

"Wait," he shrieked. "Lemme explain."

He jerked both hands back of him and upward as if trying to indicate something above.

That was a trick. It was a bit too obvious. Doc Savage spun.

Another door down the corridor behind Doc Savage had opened. A huge man, with the body of a box and a face of no intelligence, had stepped out. This one had a revolver.

Doc Savage found himself looking into the muzzle of the gun. There had been no time to do anything.

"Just hold it," said the little man who had first appeared. He now took a gun from his clothing.

Doc held it. He stood very stiffly. However, a close observer might have noted certain large arm muscles swelling in the bronze man's coat sleeve. The sinews coiled, bundled, swelled up, strained against the coat fabric.

But the two captors were too canny. They wrenched small oxygen respirators—gas mask affairs—from inside their shirts and clamped them to nostrils and lips. They must have used these previously on such occasions as the dirigible had gone so high into the stratosphere as to reach air that would not sustain human life.

Doc Savage relaxed. The big muscles in his arms subsided. These two men must know a few of his tricks. In a concealed pocket in his coat sleeve Doc Savage carried tiny glass balls of an anæsthetic which produced quick unconsciousness once it was breathed, but which lost its potency after being in the air few moments. He had been on the point of breaking the balls with his arm muscles to release the gas.

"Just one more trick," said the box of a man, "and it'll be too bad for you."

The box of a man, it was clear, was not nearly as stupid as he looked.

The two came close, but did so very carefully. Their hands snaked into Doc's pockets, ran over his person. The hands brought nothing to light.

"Huh!" grunted the box of a man. "He don't even carry a gun."

"Don't let that fool you," muttered the other.

36

They made gestures with a plain meaning. Doc Savage turned, walked toward the control cabin. The guns made twin pressures against his back. He reached the control room, stepped inside.

A giant fire-cracker seemed to go off on top of his head.

IT WAS ONE of the few times when the bronze man came close to being taken completely by surprise. The fact that he was so nearly deceived was probably due to the noise of the dirigible's engines. This covered most of the sounds which the box of a man made as he clubbed with his gun. Not all of them, however.

Doc moved enough to evade much of the blow's force. He went down because that is what they would expect him to do, but he did not go entirely flat. While still slightly above the floor, he seemed to explode.

Spinning, Doc Savage got one of the box man's legs. He jerked. The fellow went down; but the manner of his descent furnished a surprise.

The box man was a wizard with his strength. He was uncanny. Not only did he have terrible strength, but he knew how to do fantastic things with his hands; and he was only a little slower than chain lightning.

The box man landed full on top of Doc Savage, and his blunt, stubby fingers were instantly in the bronze man's neck, exerting horrible pressure on certain particular nerves and spinal segments. His legs went around Doc's middle in a peculiar scissors which completely stopped breathing.

Doc Savage's hand gripped the man's head, twisted it one way, then the other, so rapidly that the fellow could not get strain in it, then roared bull fashion; but the fellow's neck muscles had surprising strength.

The fellow hit Doc, a very scientific blow which brought pin points of light into the bronze man's gold flaked eyes.

Doc got hit again.

The bronze man wilted. The tenseness went out of his body and arms, and his head sank until his arms touched the floor.

The box man looked very glad and his grip did not relax. He hit again and again. Then he got Doc's throat, and for long moments he kept his position, squeezing, legs crushing. Finally, he began to relax, sensing victory, and a slow grin slit his square dumb-looking countenance.

"I guess I ain't so bad," he gloated between labored breaths.

His legs loosened and he started to lift himself from Doc Savage's limp body.

Then the bronze volcano exploded. As if he had been a mere featherweight, the box man felt himself tossed into the air, slammed down with a headlock, lifted and whirled in what is commonly known as an airplane spin, a very dangerous predicament in which to be, crashed to the floor.

Doc Savage did not stand and watch. He flashed for the small man. The latter had been an observer, a gleeful one at first, a discomfited one now. He was trying to get his gun into action.

The little gunman was canny, much more canny than it appeared on the surface, as it later developed.

The fellow dropped his gun, spun and ran. He got out of the control room, banged the door behind him.

Doc did not pursue him. There was a very good reason for that. The box man had only been resting, recovering from his dazed condition. He was on his feet, roaring, berserk. The fellow charged, closed with Doc Savage and began to use more of his innumerable tricks.

THERE HAD BEEN method in the flight of the box man's small companion; but there were no observers to note that. The lean, evil-faced fellow had climbed upward to a spot immediately above the control cabin where there was a second cubicle which held the apparatus that conditioned the air in the control rooms.

The man produced a flashlight. He seemed not unfamiliar with machinery as he worked his way through the banks of mechanism, stopping beside the battery of tubes which carried the air into and out of the cabins below.

The small man began to work with valves. In a moment, the man had shut off the oxygen supply.

He hurriedly retraced his way toward the control cabin.

In the cabin, Doc Savage and the box of a man were still at it. That the bronze man was up against a very accomplished opponent was evident in several bruises which he now carried. His skin was broken in a place or two.

But the box of a man was growing weak at the knees. Shoulders hunched to protect his jaws, he sidled back and forth, striving to escape the bronze man rather than approach him. His thick arms darted out repeatedly. There was still speed in them.

Unexpectedly, Doc caught the fellow's wrists, yanked, and the man came toward him helplessly. The blocky man grasped wildly at his opponent. The next instant he was giving an excellent imitation of an attempt to stand on his own face on the floor. He never did know by just what process he had been tripped, up-ended in that fashion.

The squarish fellow rolled over. He was whipped. He made no effort to get to his feet.

Doc Savage watched warily, as if suspecting a trick. He was breathing more rapidly than usual, which was another thing that showed how strenuous the scrap had been. His physical condition was excellent.

So slowly that it was almost imperceptible, the bronze man's face began to change expression. His lips seemed to set more firmly together. For a moment, a small weird sound was audible over the moan of the engines in their special enclosed compartments. It was very vague this sound, a trilling, an uncanny note, one which defied description, except that perhaps it might be likened to the exotic noise of a wind filtering through a tropical forest.

The bronze man took two rapid strides toward the controls. Then his knees collapsed slowly. He went to the floor.

He fell almost directly before the instrument panel, one dial on which registered the air condition. The needle on the oxygen portion of this dial was over on the red section, which meant dangerously low.

Back in the cabin there was a great clamor, a beating of fists on metal, howling and shouting. Monk and Ham had been aroused; but they had found themselves locked in their compartments and the doors were solid.

The blocky man's small, wizened companion appeared, gliding toward Doc Savage's prone form. The fellow now wore his small oxygen supplying device. The man made sure Doc Savage was unconscious. Then he listened to the uproar Monk and Ham were making. That seemed to cause him to become uneasy.

The box man, the terrific fighter, was lying motionless, gasping a little. The small fellow walked over, drew a revolver, and quite casually knocked his associate senseless.

THE SMALL MAN got binoculars, peered downward through the survey port in the bottom of the control cabin. There were lights below, slightly ahead. The fellow seemed to recognize them. He grinned thinly, and immediately went to the radio apparatus.

The man was no stranger to radio, his movements proved. He studied the outfit briefly. Then, without hesitation, he turned the proper knobs, got the transmitter and receiver in operation. He took his mouth from his oxygen apparatus to speak into a small microphone.

"Reporting," he said calmly.

He turned to a certain wave-length on which there must

have been a listener. For there was no wait, no preamble whatever.

"Report," said a voice over the receiver.

"Message to the Inca in Gray," said the small man over the radio. "White Legionnaire number two reporting capture of Doc Savage's dirigible."

That was all. He waited. Several moments passed. Monk and Ham still made a great deal of noise trying to get out of their cabins, but failing. As a matter of fact, those cabins had been constructed with the idea that they possibly might serve as prison cells on occasion. Escape from them was almost impossible.

A message came over the radio. It was not in English, that message, but in a code which would have been absolutely unintelligible to a listener. The small man in the dirigible, however, seemed to understand perfectly.

"Message to Inca in Gray," he said finally. "Instructions understood."

He shut off the radio apparatus, arose from the desk and again examined Doc Savage. The bronze giant's chest was not moving. He seemed to be lifeless. Showing a callous indifference, the small man paid no attention to his late companion, the burly fellow whom he had cracked over the head.

Running now, the small man made for the portion of the dirigible where they had hidden themselves since the craft had left New York. From a spot where it had been concealed among the girders, the fellow hauled out a bundle, and this, it developed, held two articles.

One of the articles was a bomb.

The other was a parachute.

The man carried the bomb, scrambled downward, sought out the most vital part of the ship, exactly amidships. He placed his bomb, showing some knowledge of explosives in the act. A clockwork detonator was attached to the infernal machine. The man set this. Then he fled.

His hands trembled with haste as he fastened the parachute harness. Then he all but fell down into the control cabin. Light, non-shatterable glass extended all around the control cabin floor. Most of it was immovable; but there were sections on either side which could be raised, hatch fashion. The man worked at one of these, got it open.

Cold air, air many degrees below zero, rushed into the ship. The man shivered. The man thought of something, leered and hurriedly opened the other hatches. He had made it three to one that Doc Savage and the others would

40

die. There was a lack of oxygen, the bomb, and this cold, which would soon freeze them.

The man hesitated and then calmly stepped through one of the open hatches, counted the usual ten seconds very carefully, then pulled the ring of the rip cord. The chute sprouted whitely above him.

He fell very rapidly, and the clouds which had at first seemed nearly carpet smooth became rugose, nodular, a forest of bulbs and clefts of vapor.

Off ahead a short distance the clouds ended. Beyond these, so small as to be barely distinguishable, more of a blur than a definite array of dots, were the lights of Alcala, capital of Santa Amoza.

The clouds followed the man descending by parachute. The fellow was cold, stiff, in fact.

The man had been trying to glance upward, but he had long ago lost sight of the airship. Minutes passed. Again and again he stared upward. He seemed to be waiting for something.

The something, judging from his intense attitude, was slow in coming. The fellow looked worried. A frown of concern grooved his forehead.

Suddenly it came. There was a flash, distinctly lighting the clouds about him. Following that, some moments later, there was a sound remindful of a great crack and whoop and gobble of thunder. Echoes of that tremendous report romped through the cloud bank.

The man in the parachute seemed satisfied. He sighed.

He made an expert landing in a patch of tall brush which scratched him somewhat. He disengaged himself from the parachute in a great hurry. Then he scuttled away.

Chapter 7

AN OFFER TO SURRENDER

SOUNDS OF THAT titanic explosion in the sky were heard over the entire city of Alcala. It caused some thousands of people to promptly rush to their bomb-proof cellars. For aërial bombing raids were not unknown in Alcala. Others of the populace swarmed into the streets, these being sold to curiosity exceeding the demands of safety and good sense. They stared at the sky, hoping to see the spectacle of an air raid.

The observers saw what seemed to be great streamers of flame dropping through the sky, flaming fragments falling toward the earth from a tremendous height perhaps. These burned themselves out long before they reached the ground. Searchlights around Alcala pointed lean white fingers into the sky, and waved about hungrily, trying to locate possible raiding planes from Delezon. Anti-aircraft guns barked a few times. Quiet finally returned.

Under cover of the excitement, however, certain sinister movements had been going on. Various men who always kept to the darkness and took great pains that their faces should not be seen had been moving toward a certain common spot. It was not difficult for them to move about undiscovered for Alcala, after that first explosion, had been promptly darkened in anticipation of an air raid.

Almost in the shadow of the rather impressive presidential palace of President Carcetas the meeting occurred. The spot was the deserted home of a certain wealthy man who had been in sympathy with the enemy country of Delezon and had found it wise to flee some two years previously. Except for a muttering of passwords there was no other sound as the men met.

Eventually, however, there was a stir of activity, a muttering.

"The master comes," some one whispered.

"The Inca in Gray," another breathed.

A moment later, their sinister master stood among them. No *fosforos,* the little paraffin matches popular in Santa Amoza, were struck. Nor did any one thumb on a flashlight. To have done so would probably have meant prompt shooting or a knife, and it would have disclosed nothing anyway.

The Inca in Gray was disguised simply and effectively. A long shroud of gray cloth, so dark a gray that it was almost black, encased the figure from head to foot. There were no eyeholes, but the cloth of the hood was thinner so that the eyes inside could peer out through the fabric.

The Inca in Gray spoke in a voice that was painstakingly altered so as to be unrecognizable.

"Has White Legionnaire number two arrived?" was the question.

The small man who had left the bomb in Doc Savage's dirigible now stepped forward and identified himself. He launched immediately into a description of his feat.

"There was T.N.T. in that bomb," he finished, speaking Spanish with the difficulty of a man who has just learned it. "You can take all of that airship that they'll find and put it in your eye."

The Inca in Gray was ominously silent.

"A little more respect in your manner, please," said the voice back of the hood.

Although the voice of the disguised master mind was excellently disguised, a close listener might have detected one possibility. The English which the being spoke was better than the Spanish. The English words came more freely.

The assembled followers of the Inca in Gray seemed to know what they were there for. No orders were given.

The Inca in Gray simply said, "We will act now, señors."

The meeting dispersed.

THE SINISTER cloaked figure of the Inca in Gray appeared alongside the presidential palace shortly afterward. There were no lights, but sentries could be heard shifting back and forth in the darkness.

The Inca in Gray listened to the sounds the sentries made. Some moments of this was sufficient to furnish an excellent idea of the beats the fellows patrolled. The vague form that was the Inca in Gray scuttled forward.

Santa Amoza had been at war a long time; and war means that political leaders must take more than the average precautions against an assassination. President Carcetas had, as a move to protect the life of his daughter, caused a tall, thick screen of shrubbery to be thrown up around the palace verandas.

Pretty Señorita Anita Carcetas was at this moment resting herself on a veranda, where she not only was hidden from the street, but from any one in the palace grounds as well. The young woman was reading the local newspapers which were filled with the usual claims that Santa Amoza had the enemy, Delezon, practically whipped.

The young woman actually considered herself perfectly safe. If she heard a faint sound behind her, she dismissed it as being made by a servant. A large pad of cloth was over her mouth before she was aware of danger. The cloth was saturated and reeking with a well known hospital anæsthetic. The young woman struggled furiously. She could not see her captor. She kicked backward, contacted shins.

For a moment she got her face free of the wet cloth. She emitted piercing screams, and, because she had gotten a glimpse at the grim covering of her assailant, she jumped at a correct conclusion.

"The Inca in Gray!" she screamed. "Help!"

Then her attacker got the soaked cloth back over her nostrils, lifted her and carried her way. The anæsthetic had her senseless before she had been taken far.

EXCITEMENT RAN like fire through the presidential palace. Sentries dashed about. An attempt was made to turn the lights on, but it was discovered the power lines had been cut. The enforced darkness only increased the confusion.

President Carcetas of Santa Amoza dashed out of his private office. He asked questions of an excited sentry.

"Señorita Anita——"

"Carried away," the soldier blurted.

President Carcetas became very pale at that.

"Stop this wild dashing about," he roared in Spanish. "Order all streets in the vicinity of the presidential palace blocked. Have squads of soldiers search the houses. Notify the police. Quickly!"

The soldiers scurried away.

President Carcetas moved to the left wing of the presidential palace and soon stopped in front of a closed door. He lifted his hand and knocked, got no answer, knocked again. His black eyebrows ran up on his forehead. He hesitated, then turned the knob and entered.

At first glance, it appeared the room was vacant. Sheets and blankets had been thrown back from the bed, as if it had been slept in. A taboret near the head of the bed was upset. A glass of water that had been on it had wetted the carpet.

A groan sounded. It was muffled.

President Carcetas's eyebrows ran down, then up, and he sprang forward, hot lights in his piercing eyes. He sank beside the bed, looked under it, and a moment later pulled a bound figure into view. The fellow was gagged, but removal of this speech impediment took only a moment.

The bound man who had been under the bed was long and lean. The hair on his bullet-shaped head was close cropped.

The man was Count Hoffe, munitions salesman. His presence at the presidential palace was no mystery. President Carcetas of Santa Amoza had been placing a new order for munitions, and terms had needed discussing. Hence, Count Hoffe had remained at the palace for the night.

"What happened?" President Carcetas demanded.

Count Hoffe groaned. An ugly bump showed on the side of his head. One of his eyes was all but closed, and a small stream of scarlet crawled from one nostril.

"A sinister figure in a gray cloak was creeping through my room." Count Hoffe explained. "When I awakened, he struck me down."

"Did you see the face of this assailant?" Carcetas asked.

Count Hoffe hesitated, moistened his lips.

"I did."

"Who was it?" President Carcetas barked.

"The information will not be pleasant," Count Hoffe mumbled. "It will be a shock."

"Who was your attacker?" the chief executive of Santa Amoza requested grimly.

"Ace Jackson," said Count Hoffe.

President Carcetas was genuinely shocked, it was plain. His jaw dropped and his eyes widened.

"Ace Jackson," he said grimly. "Are you sure?"

Count Hoffe nodded painfully. "I am sure."

"But Ace Jackson is lying in the hospital badly burned," reminded President Carcetas. "He could walk only a few paces."

Count Hoffe was free of the fastening rope now. He sat on the edge of the bed and held his head in his hands.

"You might have the hospital called to see if Ace Jackson is still there," he suggested.

President Carcetas barked an order. One of his many secretaries immediately got in touch with the hospital where Ace Jackson had been confined. The secretary came scampering back with a surprised look on his face.

"Ace Jackson is gone," he said.

"Now we know the identity of the Inca in Gray," Count Hoffe growled.

45

President Carcetas said nothing in reply. He seemed to be too deeply stricken for words.

The section of the city in which the presidential palace stood was now in an uproar. Machine guns had been erected in the streets. Lines of soldiers blocked the thoroughfares. No one was allowed to enter or leave.

Squads of soldiers were searching houses regardless of whether the occupants wanted it or not. President Carcetas dashed here and there. He waved his arms; he shrieked. His demeanor was altogether that of a man on the verge of going to pieces.

This was surprising. President Carcetas was ordinarily a taciturn man who kept his temper. Ordinarily, he never flew into rages, and because he kept his head level his decisions were usually just. This was what made him probably the most genuinely respected president Santa Amoza had ever had.

Now, however, President Carcetas was a different man. The seizing of his daughter had done that. If he remained in his present condition, he would be unfit to guide the destinies of the republic. He was, in fact, liable to commit all kinds of blunders.

"Why should the Inca in Gray seize my daughter?" he screamed repeatedly.

Count Hoffe took pains to shake his own head sorrowfully. If he had any ideas on the subject, he did not voice them.

President Carcetas snapped frightfully at those who tried to comfort him; even when an officer brought a sentry who claimed he saw a strange figure escaping the grounds.

"Did you see the individual's face?" roared President Carcetas.

"I am not sure," spoke the sentry. "But I think——"

"You think what?" Carcetas was frankly frantic.

"I think it was Señor Don Kurrell, the oil man," said the sentry.

THE EFFECT of the soldier's words was that of a minor explosion. Ominous mutters went up.

Count Hoffe, disbelief on his militaristic features, shouted, "That must be a mistake! It must have been Ace Jackson!"

"It resembled—Don Kurrell," insisted the sentry.

If President Carcetas had been imitating a madman before, he put much more zest in the performance now. He all but bowled his chief of staff over, shouting, "Get Don Kurrell! Have him brought here at once!"

Soldiers scampered out, entered fast official cars, and these

46

roared away. It was well known that Don Kurrell maintained a suite in Alcala's finest hotel.

Within twenty minutes, the officer in charge of the soldiers sent to get Don Kurrell telephoned. He was speaking from Kurrell's hotel.

"Don Kurrell has not been seen all evening," he reported.

President Carcetas went into a fresh spasm at this. He ordered guards all over the city quadrupled. He directed that the airport be watched, the trains be searched, that all automobiles be stopped and thoroughly examined.

Official cars had been making a great deal of noise in their going and coming, but this was nothing to the uproar of sirens which now accompanied the arrival of an expensive foreign limousine, trailed by four military automobiles bearing a personal bodyguard of soldiers. There was a coat of arms on the foreign limousine for every one to see and thereby know who rode within.

Señor Junio Serrato, minister of war, commander in chief of the armies of Santa Amoza, was the man who was second in power to President Carcetas. War minister Serrato's face wore a worried look as he alighted and dashed into the presidential palace.

He got a jarring greeting from President Carcetas.

"Where have you been?" howled the chief executive of Santa Amoza. "When I need you, you are not around!"

"Shut up!" said war minister Serrato, with equal brusqueness. "Read this. It was shoved under the door of my home."

Serrato presented a folded paper for the other's inspection.

To be delivered to President Carcetas:
Your daughter is by now in my hands. In the room next to her a firing squad will be oiling rifles. Whether or not the girl stands before this firing squad depends on President Carcetas. If Santa Amoza surrenders to Delezon, the girl will be released unharmed. If there is no surrender, she will, I can assure you, be shot.
General Fernanez Vigo,
Dictator General of Delezon.

President Carcetas' hands seemed to die in a limp way. The paper dropped from his hands to the floor.

"Vigo—has—Anita!" he gasped.

War minister Serrato, his Latin handsomeness somewhat stark, made a grim mouth. He rubbed a fingernail over the thin line of his black mustache.

"What moves shall we make?" he asked.

47

President Carcetas drew himself up. He was very pale as if about to faint.

"Order an unconditional surrender immediately!" he snapped.

War minister Serrato's mustache jerked a little. Determination came over his face, settled there so heavily that it made his features almost ugly.

"No!" he snarled. "Santa Amoza will never surrender!"

TENSION CAME into the room, a tension which was as real and which affected every one as if it had been a cold wind. There were present a number of old generals who had been through revolutions before the day of President Carcetas. These canny old fellows drew to one side and dropped hands to the guns which they wore at their belts. They became expectant, tense.

President Carcetas was glaring at war minister Serrato. The chief executive of Santa Amoza looked somewhat stunned, and, for a moment, his calmness was almost deadly.

"You heard my orders," he said grimly. "We surrender."

"I heard your orders," minister Serrato told him. "We do not surrender!"

President Carcetas blew up.

"You are no longer a war minister!" He turned to the soldiers and screamed, "Arrest this man!"

The officers present had obeyed President Carcetas for a long time. Habit got the best of them. They moved forward.

War minister Junio Serrato drew himself up. His little mustache was a straight line, and he now made a speech that went down in Santo Amoza history.

"Wait!" he said. "The future of Santa Amoza depends on what we do within the next few moments. The situation which confronts you has behind it, I believe, more than meets the eye. I refer, of course, to the sinister depredations of this mysterious fiend known as the Inca in Gray."

War minister Serrato paused to look over the assemblage. They had stopped, were listening to him.

"The Inca in Gray has seized Señorita Anita Carcetas," Serrato continued quietly. "There was a purpose behind that seizure, a purpose that is plain. The purpose is about to be accomplished. President Carcetas is a man whom we all love and revere and respect, but he is not himself now. He is a man driven insane by danger threatening the one he loves. I do not censure him for that. No one can. But I do not think you, the generals who have fought with me, or I, should permit the surrender of Santa Amoza. For that is obviously the thing the Inca in Gray intended to happen."

That was all he said, but it was enough to make the others think. It was a crucial moment. President Carcetas did the thing which really swayed the course of action.

Waving his arms, screaming shrilly, President Carcetas shouted, "Santa Amoza must surrender! The life of my daughter depends upon it!"

That decided the assembled generals. Thousands of men had already died in the war. It was a terrible decision which confronted them, but they, as soldiers, saw their way clear. The life of one person, even of attractive Señorita Anita Carcetas, must not lose everything for Santa Amoza.

President Carcetas was seized. They carried him, screaming, gibbering to a secluded portion of the presidential palace.

Señor Junio Serrato looked on quietly. If there was elation in his heart, he hid it. He did not look like a man who had just become actual ruler of Santa Amoza.

Count Hoffe, munitions salesman, had been an obscure on-looker. Count Hoffe had taken pains to stand well in the rear, but it was purely by chance he positioned himself near a tapestry. He had paid no attention to that tapestry. When a voice now reached his ears, he did not, at first, realize it was coming from behind the hanging.

"You have just witnessed a rather unusual revolution," said the voice, which was low and cultured. "Should war minister Junio Serrato himself be the Inca in Gray, he could not have planned more skillfully. By this one stroke, he has made himself all powerful in Santa Amoza."

Now this speech was one which might well prove not to be the healthiest of utterances. Men have been shot for less.

Count Hoffe turned to see who had spoken. His eyes flew wide. He actually jumped some inches off the floor.

"Doc Savage!" he squawked.

Chapter 8

SABOTAGE

COUNT HOFFE's shout was very loud and very surprised. It promptly drew all eyes to the giant bronze man who had just stepped from behind the tapestry, which, incidentally, covered a window that admitted to the palace grounds.

No one said anything for several moments. Perhaps the silence was due in part to the impressive presence of the bronze man. For, as he stood there, his giant size, the strange power in his flake gold eyes, his combination of bronze skin and slightly darker bronze hair, were very impressive.

War minister Junio Serrato stepped forward. His thin mustache warped a smile. He executed a brisk bow.

"Santa Amoza is honored," he said. "May we hope that you had an interesting trip down?"

"It proved to be interesting enough," Doc Savage said dryly.

War minister Serrato caught the double meaning, promptly demanded, "What do you mean?"

Doc Savage was a student of human nature, and knew a great deal about the most effective methods of going about obtaining his ends. A frank statement of his position frequently avoided misunderstanding and difficulties. So he told exactly what had happened including the attempt on his life in New York and ending with the dirigible flight southward after he had learned Long Tom was missing. He described the fight in the dirigible. That part was interesting.

The airship control cabin, it seemed, was equipped with emergency oxygen appartus, which went into operation automatically when the main source of supply failed. The emergency equipment had saved Doc Savage's life. In fact, he had only been unconscious for a brief period, reviving in time to observe the small man leaping with the parachute.

A hasty search had located the bomb, and it had required no great skill to disconnect the clockwork mechanism so that the infernal machine would not explode.

"We carried the thing to a hatch, reset the clock mechanism and tossed it overboard," Doc explained. "It went off in the air, far below us. That was to lead the would-be killer to think his plot had succeeded."

"Where is your dirigible?" war minister Serrato asked.

"In the stratosphere above Alcala," Doc explained. "It seemed advisable to let our mysterious enemies think we were dead. An auxiliary plane brought me down to earth. Monk and Ham are with the dirigible."

"You say you employed—an auxiliary plane?" War minister Serrato seemed puzzled.

"A very small craft carried inside the dirigible," Doc told him. "Not a new procedure, as you may know."

"Where did you leave the plane?" the other queried.

"At a small airport west of the city," Doc replied.

War minister Serrato smiled slightly, but without humor. "You got past the presidential palace guards quite easily."

"They nearly caught me several times," Doc corrected.

Serrato seemed to be considering that. When it became apparent that he was to have nothing more to say on the subject, Doc Savage spoke.

"Long Tom—Major Thomas J. Roberts," the bronze man reminded. "His whereabouts is the most important thing to me at present."

War minister Serrato looked grim at that, his mustache an upside down arc. "We have, as you might expect, an espionage system in the enemy country of Delezon."

Doc Savage's flake gold eyes were steady. "And your spies have reported what?"

"That Señor Long Tom Roberts was yesterday shot as a spy," Serrato said.

DOC SAVAGE'S expression, strangely enough, did not alter in the slightest at that; but a moment after he had heard the news concerning Long Tom, there was a sound in the room, a small eerie mysterious sound, a trilling. It might have been the note of some fantastic tropical songster, so vague that it all but defied recognition, and possessed of a ventriloquial quality which made it seem to come from everywhere. It trailed up and down some vagrant scale of its own and died away.

"This report was reliable?" he asked.

"Quite," war minister Serrato nodded. "There's not the slightest doubt."

"Tell me what you know of this Inca in Gray," the bronze man suggested abruptly.

War minister Serrato blinked, then replied. The bronze man listened silently to the review of the sometimes rather horrible activities which were delineated. The tale told a very definite story of its own. Time after time the Inca in Gray had smashed offensives which had seemed certain to give victory to Santa Amoza.

51

"That makes it seem as if the Inca in Gray were a representative of your enemy, Delezon," Doc suggested.

War minister Serrato nodded his head. "We have thought so, but there has never been proof."

Doc Savage said nothing more, but turned toward the door.

"What do you plan?" Serrato demanded.

"A visit to General Fernanez Vigo, general dictator of Delezon," Doc Savage said.

The other's thin mustache was a rapidly bending line. "But——"

"General Vigo executed Long Tom," Doc said quietly. There was no rage in the bronze man's voice, no crashing wrath; but the controlled tones held something else, held a quality so chilling, so determined that war minister Serrato took a step backward. He bowed.

"The facilities of Santa Amoza are at your disposal," he said.

"Thank you." The bronze man hesitated. "My preference is to work alone."

He stepped through the same window by which he had arrived, and, although there were guards in the grounds, and in the surrounding streets, his departure was undiscovered. The bronze man was a master of stealth, a wizard at going places without being seen.

There were a few lights along the streets of Alcala now. The night was hot, and even a military edict could not keep doors shut and windows shuttered. Even an excellent system of street-lighting, however, would not have made the avenues of Alcala, especially in the poorer section, easily traversed after nightfall. Over in the old town, on the west side, streets were all narrow, and, more often than not, rough, some lined with débris.

Could an observer have noted the progress of the bronze man, that person would perhaps have sworn that Doc had the eyes of a cat. As a matter of fact, the bronze man possessed something better than that.

He wore goggles of peculiar construction—they had lenses complex, fully as large as condensed-milk cans. In one hand he carried a box of a device which resembled an oversized magic lantern. The lens of this was very large and almost intensely black. It seemed to give off no light—which was deceptive. The box was a lantern for the projection of light rays outside the visible spectrum, and the goggles, amazingly complex, made it possible for the bronze man to see with this unusual light.

Hence, although he traveled through what was apparently

52

intense darkness, he could actually see with fair distinctness what went on about him.

Running easily, he sped through the streets, dodging obstructions, making fast time toward the small airport on the outskirts of the city. He was careful to keep clear of pedestrains, and when he saw cars coming he ducked into darkened doorways.

He reached the airport. He came on the scene silently, using the "black light" lantern. That accounted for the fact that he took a number of men by surprise.

THERE WERE SEVEN of them. They wore civilian garments, and it was necessary to no more than look at them to understand why they wore such clothing. A recruiting officer, even in war time, would hesitate to pass such ugly looking specimens as these.

They drew near the plane. Without seeming to change his stride, Doc Savage's speed increased. He made no noise. Although he could see clearly, there was intense darkness around the little airport, and the eyes of the men, of course, failed to register the presence of the black light.

Doc Savage closed in, on the rearmost. He could hear them talking.

"Hurry, *amigos*," the one who seemed to be in charge was saying. "There is little time."

"Why does the Inca in Gray wish the plane destroyed?" one muttered.

"That is the question of a child," sniffed the other. "Have you not heard of the aërial push against Delezon, which Ace Jackson this afternoon ordered from his hospital bed?"

"I heard many planes in the air," one grunted.

"There are no other aircraft in Alcala for Doc Savage to use," said the first speaker. "Hence, if we destroy this ship, he will have to remain in Alcala."

That was not all Doc Savage would have preferred to hear, but they were starting to wreck the ship. That would have to be stopped. The bronze man drove out a beam of an arm. A man moaned, dropped under the blow.

Doc Savage picked up the fallen fellow as though he were weightless, and whirled him, club fashion. When he released him, two more men were bowled over.

Doc Savage whipped backward, making no noise, circling. He still held the black light lantern, but now he placed this on the ground, its rays playing on the group about the plane. Then he charged.

53

A man tried to drag out a flashlight. Doc went to him, clipped him alongside the temple. The fellow fell.

The survivors were shouting, charging about madly, falling over the fallen forms of their companions.

One, by the rankest of good luck, got a grip around Doc's neck. The bronze man reached back, grasped his assailant, whipped him swiftly. The man screamed in the air. The shriek was ended with a hollow, unpleasant sound as his body hit the ground.

There were two survivors now, and they got frightened. They put their heads back, their chests out, and ran. Nature probably invented fear as a stimulant to make her children move swiftly when there is need to do so. These men were frightened, and thought death was at their heels, and they probably ran faster than they ever had before.

Doc Savage was delayed a moment when one of the men who had already gone down in the fight strove to get to his feet. He sank when Doc Savage clipped his jaw, and remained down, only breathing showing that he was alive.

Doc Savage pursued the two who had fled. Fast as these two traveled, Doc Savage was swifter. He did not, however, catch them until they had covered all of two hundred yards. The breath was coming out of their lungs with whistles like the barking of small dogs.

He felled them as they ran by pulling up alongside them and using his fists. The first sank easily. The second made a ball out of himself and went head over heels with a loud slopping noise.

Doc Savage was examining them when he heard a plane motor roar into life.

DOC SAVAGE straightened, listened. It was a plane, certainly. Its roar was coming from back at the field. There was a bass crash of power about the motor that enabled Doc to recognize it instantly—his own plane!

The bronze man ran toward the field. What had happened was unexpected. The men he had left there, his assailants—six out of the eight—would certainly still be senseless. He knew how hard he had struck them.

Doc was heading for the unusual lantern which projected the black light, and which he had left on the ground at the scene of the fight. He found it, picked it up, and twisted a rheostat on it making the beam stronger. Ordinarily, he did not use it full strength, because the small, powerful batteries would be quickly exhausted. He doubled around shrubbery, raced through a clump of palm trees, and the invisible rays from his lantern picked up the plane.

54

The ship was in motion, traveling rather fast, wavering a little uncertainly. Palm trees lined the opposite side of the field. Straight for these the little all-metal craft scudded.

With devastating force the ship hit the palms. Wings snapped off. The motor left the craft and went on ahead like a bullet. There was a spectacular crash, a *whoosh!* as the gasoline caught. The flames spread, not only enwrapping what was left of the plane, but climbing the palm trees and turning them into pillars of fire.

Doc Savage did not go toward the ship; it was ruined, of course.

The bronze man had kept on running throughout the whole thing. He merely changed his course now, veering toward the spot where he had left the six unconscious men. His strange light device picked them up an instant later. He counted, all six of them. They were exactly as he had left them.

But no! Not as he had left them. They had been alive.

Now they were dead.

Doc Savage was still using the black light. The aspect of things, as viewed with this light was somewhat unnatural, high-lights and shadows being more starkly emphasized; but it was certain that the six were dead.

There was something else also, a weird appearance of the skin, a vague glow somewhat like phosphorescence. Doc Savage switched off the light, removed the goggles, and extracted a small flashlight from his clothing. He thumbed it on.

The instant he looked at the six dead men his strange trilling came into existence. The sound seemed smaller, more eerie than ever, and it persisted only a moment.

A grayish powder covered the hands, the faces of the dead men. The stuff might have been an unclean dust.

The mark of death by the hand of the Inca in Gray!

Doc Savage went swiftly to a knee. Reaching into a pocket, he extracted an envelope, not an ordinary paper envelope, but one of a varnished silk, both water and air proof.

He did not touch the powder, but with blades of grass brushed some of it into the envelope. He rolled the top of the envelope tightly and fitted over it a metal clamp, which rendered it air-tight. He pocketed this.

He had been listening; and now he heard the sound he had expected to hear. A man moving.

Doc Savage advanced toward the sound. He made no effort to move noiselessly, but his progress was almost silent.

55

His keen ears caught the sound of more motion ahead of him. Some one was creeping away.

Doc donned the goggles, turned the infra-light projector on again. The invisible rays—invisible to the unaided eye—disclosed no one. The skulker was inside the undergrowth which surrounded the field.

Doc Savage decreased his speed slightly as he entered the growth. That was necessary to maintain silence. He heard his quarry more often. The fellow seemed to be moving faster, attempting to get away from the vicinity.

With a burst of speed that was a bit dazzling, had there been light to observe it, Doc Savage shot forward. He discerned a crouching, running figure. The marauder was quickly overhauled.

The bronze man struck no blow. He merely grasped the fugitive's arms just above the wrists, lifted the fellow and slammed him to the hard ground.

They remained thus an instant. Neither spoke. Neither moved. Then Doc Savage transferred both the fellow's wrists to the vise grip of one bronze hand, and with the other hand extracted his electric flashlight and brushed off the goggles. He switched the flash on.

The captive was a tall angular mummy of bandages. He had a face that looked as if it had gone through many a fight. His nose was particularly flat, giving his countenance the aspect of an English bulldog.

The captive grinned widely.

"I've heard a lot about you," he said. "An' I'll tell the wide-eyed world that you live up to advance notices."

"Who," Doc Savage asked, "are you?"

"Ace Jackson," the prisoner said.

Chapter 9

CRACK-UP

Doc Savage's fingers, clamping the man's wrists, did not loosen. The grip was tight and painful. The grin disappeared from Ace Jackson's face and he writhed a little.

"Take it easy," he requested. "After all, I'm supposed to be an invalid."

Doc Savage suddenly slapped Ace Jackson's arm and chest lightly. He slapped numerous spots. Only twice did the flyer wince.

"You are supposed to be very badly burned," Doc Savage told him. "Actually, you seem to be in fair condition."

Ace Jackson flushed, quite distinctly. He moistened his lips; he wrinkled the flat nose that gave his face the bulldog aspect.

"Lookit," he muttered. "If you had a pretty girl who came to see you every day and held your hand and stuff like that, wouldn't a hospital look pretty good to you? Fact is I coulda been out two weeks ago, but I been doing a little faking."

Doc Savage said nothing, looked at the man. Ace Jackson grinned wisely, plainly hoping his story would be believed.

"That's straight," insisted the flyer. "But, for gosh sake don't tell Anita."

"What were you doing here?" Doc Savage asked abruptly.

"I was following a guy," said Ace Jackson.

"Who?"

"Don Kurrell," Ace Jackson grunted.

"You suspect him, too?" Doc queried.

"I'm a very suspicious guy," said Ace Jackson. "And I suspect everybody. The plain nasty truth is I haven't got ideas enough to suspect anybody in particular."

"Granted that Don Kurrell is the Inca in Gray," Doc Savage said, "what would be his motive?"

"Plenty," said Ace Jackson. "He's an oil man. These oil guys pull all kinds of stunts. He may have a deal with old General Vigo of Delezon whereby, if Vigo whips Santa Amoza, Don Kurrell's company gets oil concessions in the combined republics."

"Any proof of that?" Doc asked.

"Nope," Ace Jackson admitted. "But you never can tell."

A hoarse scream sounded suddenly, startlingly. It was wordless, but it did not need words. It was a plea for help. Ace Jackson leaped erect, although his wrists were still in Doc Savage's grip. They moved toward the source of the scream, and Doc Savage still held the flyer.

They could hear a body plunging through the undergrowth, undoubtedly the one who had screamed. The fellow was coming toward them. He came into view an instant later.

He was a short plump man, and, when he saw them and stopped, he did a small peculiar thing, evidently a habitual mannerism. He drew himself up on tiptoes, as if to look taller.

"Don Kurrell!" Ace Jackson barked.

Doc Savage's flake-gold eyes appraised Don Kurrell. There was nothing particularly distinguishing about the small man who represented a European oil concern, except his diminutive size and his small efforts to make himself appear as large as other men.

"What is wrong?" Doc Savage asked.

Don Kurrell took hold of the bronze man's arm as if to draw strength and encouragement from the contact.

"You are Doc Savage?" he gasped. "I've heard much of you, have seen your pictures."

"What is wrong?" the bronze man repeated.

"The Inca in Gray is trying to kill me," Kurrell gulped.

"Just now?" Doc queried.

"Twice," Don Kurrell said rapidly. "Once at my hotel, when I escaped. I started to go to the presidential palace, but on the way I heard soldiers talking. I learned that I was suspected—the Señorita Anita Carcetas had been kidnaped, and I was accused."

When he heard the words stating that Señorita Anita Carcetas had been kidnaped, Ace Jackson looked as if he had been struck with a whip. He seemed too stunned to speak. If it was acting, it was good.

Don Kurrell continued rapidly, "I also overheard the soldiers say that your plane was here. So I came to head you off to talk with you. I need your help. I want you to clear me. I'm in deadly danger."

"Why should the Inca in Gray try to kill you?" Doc Savage queried.

"I do not know," Don Kurrell said. "That is absolutely true. I do not know. And this other thing, this charge of making away with the girl. Why, they may shoot me on the mere circumstantial evidence of that soldier's word that the man looked like myself."

Ace Jackson screamed suddenly, "Anita gone! You did it!"

The flyer wrenched free of Doc Savage and pitched himself headlong at Don Kurrell. He was so much larger than the oil representative, so much more of a fighter that he would have made short shrift of his victim; but Doc Savage got between them, did things with his arms and one leg, and Ace Jackson was suddenly flat on his back, gasping for breath.

Ace Jackson screamed, "Damn him! He's the Inca in Gray!"

SILENCE FOLLOWED that, an interval during which Ace Jackson's hysterical shout seemed to echo through the night.

Don Kurrell retreated a step as if the very force of the accusation had knocked him back. Next he did a quite senseless thing. He began to brush his bedraggled clothes. He was not trying to make himself look tall now. He seemed very small, almost pitiful.

"You—why I——" Suddenly he straightened. Up on his tiptoes he went. He drove an arm out rigidly at Ace Jackson.

"You!" he barked. "Why haven't I really thought of you before?" Excitement made him almost inarticulate.

"Meaning what?" Doc Savage asked abruptly.

"Meaning that I should have thought of Ace Jackson before," Don Kurrell snapped. "He is a paid war pilot, a mercenary, and he always seems to be on or near the scene when the Inca in Gray is active. He is the man who kills with the strange gray dust. He is the man who had Señorita Anita Carcetas kidnaped. Ace Jackson is the Inca in Gray!"

Ace Jackson stood and took the accusation, but his bull-dog face was purpled and his mouth worked strangely.

Doc Savage's flake-gold eyes missed no move of the little tableau. If he believed one or the other of these two, his expression betrayed no evidence of the fact.

"Can either of you men prove your opinions?" Doc asked. They only glared. It was plain they could not.

Doc Savage grasped each by the arm and hurried them through the undergrowth. They reached the spot where the other two members of the party of eight, which Doc had overpowered, had been left.

The two forms were still on the ground. Ace Jackson looked at the pair and emitted a sharp gasp. Don Kurrell, looking also, seemed to lose some inches of his hard-fought-for stature.

The two were dead, horribly so. On all parts of their exposed skin the grisly gray dust, which was the special mark of the death of the Inca in Gray, lay filmed.

Doc Savage separated Don Kurrell and Ace Jackson, released them, then bent over the two bodies. There had been no time to search the others, but there was opportunity to examine these. The bronze man went over them carefully, wearing rubber gloves, which he drew from a pocket, and which he carried for numerous purposes—handling electric wires, leaving no fingerprints, working with chemicals. Removal of the victims' clothing uncovered no marks that might have brought death. Yet, their features were contorted, their eyes staring and hideous. Death, when it had come upon them even while they were unconscious, had been no pleasant thing.

The examination took some time, and when it was over, Doc Savage guided Don Kurrell and Ace Jackson back to the tarmac of the flying field. There they all got a surprise.

A flashlight blazed unexpectedly.

"What seems to be happening here, Señor Savage?" said a smooth voice.

War minister Junio Serrato stepped from the shadows. When Doc had last seen him, the war minister of Santa Amoza had been neat and immaculate; but now he was somewhat disheveled. He had perspired. He wore no coat. There was dirt on his shoes, and his hair, and one trouser leg.

The man evidently seemed to think some accounting for his appearance was due.

"I came to the airport to see that you got away safely," he said. "I saw the burning plane. I tried to extinguish the flames, but unsuccessfully."

Doc Savage did not nod. Nor yet did he show in any way that he might disbelieve the story.

"Your guards came with you?" the bronze man asked.

"I came alone," said war minister Serrato. "It was quicker."

The manner in which he snapped out the words gave a hint that the questioning was not exactly welcome.

Doc Savage's metallic eyes sought the sky, which seemed perceptibly lighter. Dawn was coming.

"There are no planes at all available in Alcala?" he murmured questioningly.

"Correct." War minister Serrato scowled at Ace Jackson.

"This man ordered all planes to the front. He did so without consulting me."

Ace Jackson put out his jaw and said, "The air force of Santa Amoza is a separate unit. That was my understanding when I took it over. What I say goes, and I don't have to ask anybody."

War minister Serrato smiled much too grimly and said, "It is possible that arrangement will be changed."

Ace Jackson snorted. He turned to Doc Savage.

"There's one plane here," he said. "It ain't such a hot bus. It's my old barnstorming Jenny that I flew up here in. But it's here and you're welcome to it."

"Take me to it," Doc Savage requested.

The bronze man walked away from the others, went to a clump of brush at the edge of the field. He took from the brush a small bag which he had concealed there when he first arrived in his own plane. Carrying the bag, Doc walked back to the others.

War minister Serrato, it developed, had a car waiting some distance away. They went to the machine and Serrato drove.

Doc Savage rode in front, and shortly war minister Serrato found occasion to lean over and whisper in his ear, "Don Kurrell and Ace Jackson—each accused the other of being the Inca in Gray. What do you wish done about that?"

"Nothing," Doc Savage said.

War minister Serrato swore expressively under his breath and said, "If it is vaguely possible that either of those señores is the Inca in Gray, I will have them both shot."

"No," Doc Savage said.

DOC SAVAGE said nothing when he saw Ace Jackson's old Jenny. Probably that indicated as much as anything that had gone before just how great was the bronze man's self-control. The Jenny was an airplane, although there might have been some who would have looked at it and promptly made denial. In contrast to the sleek streamlining of Doc's little ship that had been destroyed, this one gave the impression of a slow moving and clumsy snail.

In comparison with a modern fighting ship, this crate looked as antique as the glorified kite with which the Wrights had startled the world at Kittyhawk.

Doc Savage checked the engine. It was old, but had recently been overhauled. It might hold together. He put the small bag behind the stick.

There was nothing decrepit about the machine gun, however. This was nearly new, and modern as they came, and the ammo belts were fully charged. Doc removed the canvas cover and checked this also. It was on a scarf ring. No Bowden control wires to rust out in the tropical dampness. You simply pulled the trigger. It was not synchronized to shoot through the prop.

"With cowl guns sunk through the prop, you gotta aim at your ship," Ace Jackson explained. "You're damn lucky to keep this old hen in the air, much less aim her at anything."

Ace Jackson whirled the prop. Doc shouted, "Contact." The motor gave one loud bark and stopped. They tried again. It caught, banged and whanged and shook the whole ship. Dust and leaves fell off the wings.

Doc Savage looked at the instrument panel. Bullets had done for the altimeter some time in the past. The tachometer read thirty-three hundred, which was obviously a lie. The oil gauge was knocked out entirely.

"You just smell of her," Ace Jackson explained. "When she begins to stink, she's too hot. An' you look around for a place to squat."

"Pull the chocks," Doc Savage requested.

Ace Jackson got the blocks from under the wheels. He had to squall to make his voice heard over the motor racket.

"Good luck!" he said.

The ramshackle motor barked harder. The ship seemed to try to shake itself to pieces, after which it moved forward, gathered speed. Doc went forward with the stick, and began to think the tail would never come up. Then the bus was off. Doc banked. The plane went back over the little field, sounding like a boiler factory.

Of those looking on, Ace Jackson alone knew that they had just seen something of a miracle.

"For the love of little billygoats!" Ace Jackson gulped. "That guy's a wizard. He got her off with a fourth of the run I usually have to take."

That, coming from Ace Jackson, was a compliment indeed.

Doc Savage gave the throttle more notches, which, if it did nothing else, made the motor more noisy. He held the stick back in a steady climb. When Ace Jackson had said the old ship's ceiling was enough to clear barbwire fences, he had exaggerated a little, but not much.

Doc Savage glanced upward. But the light of dawn is tricky. There were a few clouds. He failed to see his stratosphere dirigible, which was not unexpected. The airship was probably up there higher than any modern commercial plane could rise.

Doc Savage experimented with the throttle. He lashed the stick, climbed up and did things with the carburetor so that the motor lost some of its racket and settled down to something vaguely resembling a hum. Its performance now would have astounded the already surprised Ace Jackson. The old ship had found its master.

The craft also gathered more altitude. The sun came up, and the height of the plane saved Doc from feeling the sudden terrific heat that daylight brought; but he knew the tropics, and the green jungle below was deceptive in its appearance of coolness.

But the jungle did not extend far. Ahead there was desert, spotted with scrawny bushes and out in that was a line of haze, a vague transparent rope. Doc Savage had seen battle lines before. This was the front. The haze was dust stirred up by big shells. Some of it was the smoke of battle of which poets write. Before long he could discern tiny lines dug into the blistering soil. The trenches.

Unexpectedly, a rattling, snarling and jarring sounded from the left wing bank of the ship. Doc looked. Splinters were falling off the wing. Fabric was peeling back.

He had seen that phenomena before, too. Machine-gun bullets.

THE BRONZE MAN was no stranger to bird battling tactics. He acted before he looked, booting the rudder, slanting the stick. His ancient chariot seemed to grunt and slide sideways. It got out of the lead storm.

Doc glanced upward then. Three planes were attacking him. They had come out of the sun, and it was no reflection on his ability that they had taken him unawares. The human eye is not made that can look into the sun and pick up a plane.

They were modern, foreign built, these attacking ships. They came down like buzzing meteors. One held its course. The other two angled out.

If Ace Jackson's old Jenny had behaved surprisingly well before, it began to perform miracles now. It rolled, went into a slip, then a dive, and suddenly a perfect Immelmann turn. The three attacking ships popped past while their pilots stared in surprise.

Doc Savage looked closely at them. He saw enough to tell him what he wanted to know. War planes of Delezon and Santa Amoza would be marked. These carried no identification whatever.

Doc took the right-hand ship. Out of its Immelmann the old Jenny curled half over and seemed to wiggle itself into a groove. Bronze fingers wrenched the machine gun around on its scarf ring. A little redbird seemed to perch on its muzzle and sing with a voice of thunder. Every fifth bullet was a tracer. That helped; but it did not account for the wizardry of the shooting. Only iron nerve, alloyed muscles and much practice could account for that.

Motor cowling fell off the enemy ship. The propeller lost a blade, only one blade, which was more unfortunate for a ship with a racing motor. It tore itself from its mount, or almost so, before the pilot could shut it off. It hung like a thick scab on the snout of the plane as the craft gyrated downward. The pilot lost control, then regained it. He should be able to manage a landing he could walk away from.

The outcome of the scrap surprised the other two planes. Doc Savage was close to them before they could get their wits together. They banked furiously, evaded him. Their ships had cowl guns. That was a handicap, perhaps not in ordinary bird battling, but certainly against a marksman of the bronze man's ability.

The two ships flew side by side while the pilots thought of ways and means. Then Doc Savage did something that looked foolish. He executed a manœuvre that put him directly ahead of the two planes, below them. All they had to do was dive, riddle him.

They sloped down to get their meat. The pilots were excited, eager. There was a moment when they could not see the Jenny, the old ship being below the noses of their war craft. During that moment when he was out of sight, Doc Savage doubled over, got something from a small bag which he had placed beside the control stick. The objects resembled grenades. And after he threw them over they did explode, but softly. They threw off not chilling fragments of steel, but a bluish vapor.

Doc Savage threw the old plane into the beginning of what an expert might well have sworn would be suicide manœuvre—an outside loop; but he rolled as he went into it, down and under.

The two attacking ships followed him. Both were confident. Probably they never saw the small clouds of blue vapor. These had widened, spreading rapidly. The planes flew into them.

Both motors stopped, not together, yet not more than thirty seconds apart.

Doc Savage looked back and saw the propellers come to a standstill. His metallic face held no expression. The grenades he had thrown had contained a highly expanding gas.

This stuff had been drawn into the motors of the two attackers. It had simply caused a chemical reaction which had rendered the gasoline mixtures non-explosive. Both engines would have to be thoroughly cleaned before they would run again, since the vapor would congeal on carburetor intakes and cylinder walls.

The pilots of the two planes promptly nosed down. They were in no danger, provided they could find a spot for a dead-stick landing.

Doc followed them down. His assailants, there was more than slight reason to believe, might be killers dispatched by the Inca in Gray. What else could account for the planes bearing no markings? Doc Savage intended to land to question the fellows.

But the occupants of the three planes had other ideas. They worked furiously at their cowl machine guns. These, it developed, were of a type which could be dismounted quickly. They rested them over the fuselage and began firing. They were not bad gunners. Their lead scabbed fabric off the Jenny.

Doc Savage banked away like a hawk grown suddenly wary. Then he made a most unwelcome discovery.

His gasoline tank had been punctured.

HE GOT THE JENNY clear of the open space where the three planes had landed. Then he stood up in the cockpit and looked about for a suitable spot to set his own ship down. There was none nearer than several miles. The brush below was a scrawny thick mat patch on the edge of the desert.

The planes had moved a good bit during the sky fight. They had crossed the lines. This spot was well in Delezon territory.

Doc Savage reached his decision in short order. Trying to make a landing back in the clearing in the face of those machine guns would be suicide. He straightened the ship out, pointed it for the nearest patch of desert, and lashed the stick.

Scrambling forward, he hung in what for anything less than muscles of trained metal would have been an extremely dangerous position. He tore away fabric, got at the gas tank. The hole was large and it was too late to do much about it. Most of the gasoline was gone. Doc stuffed a handkerchief in the aperture the bullets had made.

The engine began to cough, sputter. The Jenny grew logy. Then its nose went down. It was like a stricken bird. There were moments when it seemed the bronze man would not make it; but he was successful. Onto the desert at the edge of the growth he settled. There was soft sand, no helping that. The old tires rolled on top for awhile; then they went in.

The ancient Jenny grunted, did a stand on her nose. There was a loud crash as she broke her back and the wings went off. Fine sand in a cloud enveloped everything.

Chapter 10

THE KILLER LAUGHS

THERE WAS AN UPHEAVAL in the wreckage while it was still settling, and Doc Savage's head protruded from the cockpit of the broken and torn Jenny. The non-shatter glass of his goggles was crashed in, but, when he removed them, his eyes were unharmed. He stripped off his flying helmet, exposing his straight bronze hair which was like a metal skullcap. He listened.

There was shouting, but it was distant; soldiers undoubtedly. Having seen the planes come down, they would arrive before long. Doc Savage got out of the wreckage hastily. His clothing had suffered. He was cut in a place or two. He secured the bag which had been behind the control stick.

The brush had looked thick from the air, but it looked even more dense from the ground. Doc Savage did not dash directly into it, but walked in backwards, and he carefully erased each footprint which he left in the sand. This required some moments, for he did a thorough job.

The voices were coming closer. Their barkings were in Spanish. Doc grasped the boughs of a small tree, swung up, whipped to another with the accomplished ease of a circus aërialist, and vanished from view.

A squad of Delezon soldiers trotted up. Dust clung to their uniforms and made mud on their sweating faces. They gathered, cackling in Spanish, about the wrecked Jenny.

The sergeant in command of the squad looked puzzled after he had made an examination. There should have been a body in that wreckage, but there manifestly was none. Scratching his head, the sergeant inspected the sand. He failed to detect a sign of footprints.

"Diablo!" he gulped. "This is strange."

The soldiers tramped into the brush—that is, they all tramped but one. This fellow was tall, heavily built, and he had avarice in his eyes. The purpose of his lagging behind soon became evident. He was after loot. He dug into the plane wreckage, striving to reach the instruments. Had he known just how worthless those instruments were, he might have been a little less ambitious.

His whole attention was concentrated on his thievery. He did not see a giant bronze figure ease out of the underbrush, tread silently through the sand toward him. He realized nothing was wrong, until he was seized from behind. Then the knowledge was a bit tardy.

The husky Delezonian soldier struggled briefly, terrifically, only to go limp, and that without as much as seeing his attacker.

Doc Savage shouldered the fellow and carried him from view. It would not do to have the marks of a dragging body found.

Minutes passed, hot, blistering minutes. Soldiers began to come from the underbrush. More than one of them was drenched with perspiration. That jungle was terrible in heat such as this. The sergeant appeared and demanded, "Find anything?"

He was assured they had not.

Then some one had a stroke of brilliance and volunteered, *"Bueno!* I have it. The pilot of this plane leaped with a parachute. Probably he leaped miles from here and the ship came on to crash."

"Si, si," agreed the sergeant. "I believe you are right. Fall in. We will continue our march."

The rest of the soldiers now came out of the jungle. Among them was the tall, heavy-set individual whose shoulders drooped slightly. This man drew only one or two glances, those casual.

He looked exactly like the soldier who had lagged behind to loot the fallen ship.

The squad of soldiers seemed to be bound back from the lines for a period of rest. They looked as if they badly needed it.

As THEY ENTERED the general headquarters village, the tall, heavy-set, stooped soldier with the squad began to loiter behind. Discipline was lax so he got away with this. It would have taken a close observer to have detected the slightest difference between this man and the one whom he resembled so closely.

They entered the squalid outer fringe of the village. The usual swarm of dogs and camp hangers-on greeted them, and discipline became even more lax. The burly soldier with the stoop fell even farther behind. His fellows drew ahead. He made no effort to overhaul them, instead he turned off abruptly into a side street.

Now his pace changed. He moved slowly, warily.

It was, however, certain that he would be challenged by the Delezon equivalent of military police. Numbers of these gentlemen, wearing their distinguishing arm bands,

68

were on the streets. Two of them, looking neat and cool despite the heat, confronted the burly soldier unexpectedly with a challenge.

The heavy, stooped soldier glared at the two M. P.s. The soldier was caked from head to foot with dust, and his visage was muddy, his eyes, habitually thin slits as if from exposure to the tropical sun. He put out a jaw at the two military policemen and sneered his contempt.

"You are looking at a man," he said belligerently. "I have fought the heat, the fever, the insects, and the enemy. I would enjoy fighting two fat old women such as yourselves. One side! Let a man pass!"

Had it been anywhere but South America, these words would have precipitated a prompt fight. As it was, the M. P.s scowled and drew aside. Not only were these soldiers returning from the front accorded extra privileges on order of General Vigo, but the hardships of the front sometimes rendered the soldiers a little mad. It was not healthy to fool with them.

The tall, heavy-set soldier went on, still with his stoop. He used somewhat more care and was not again challenged.

It was not difficult for him to locate the building used by General Vigo for headquarters. This was a large structure, evidently a private residence prior to the war. Strangely enough, it was of modernistic construction, boxlike, with very large windows.

The burly soldier loitered past the front of the headquarters. Numerous soldiers were about. He mingled with them. There seemed to be no reason why he should not do this.

But there was, it developed, a reason.

So unexpectedly that it was like lightning out of a clear sky, he was covered by rifles. Three Delezonian officers had suddenly presented the weapons, muzzles first. The pieces were cocked. The burly soldier lost a little of his stoop, blinked foolishly at the guns and the men who held them.

"Would you please try to escape, señor?" invited one of the officers.

The burly soldier ignored the invitation. He merely continued his dumb blinking.

"Take him to General Vigo," directed one of the officers.

GENERAL FERNANEZ VIGO, general dictator of Delezon, had appropriated for his office what had once been the sunroom of the modernistic house which was so out of place in this humble village.

General Vigo was walking angry circles around a shiny

glass and chromium table, putting each foot down with a violence that shook the floor. General Vigo wore two pistols and a bayonet. His uniform, which bore no insignia, was torn and ripped in several places. There was a bandage around his head, and another around one arm. That very afternoon General Vigo had personally led a charge into the Santa Amoza trenches.

General Vigo managed to do a spectacular thing such as this occasionally. It inspired his soldiers, probably accounted for the good showing which Delezon, a potentially weaker country than Santa Amoza, had made in the war thus far.

General Vigo stopped his pacing when the prisoner was brought into his presence.

"*Bueno!*" he howled. "One of you we have finally captured!"

The prisoner executed several snappy salutes and gulped, "I do not understand."

"Oh, yes, you do!" roared General Vigo. "I ordered your detachment of soldiers back from the front especially so that you could be arrested. You slipped away from the squad, and we thought you had become suspicious. But no, you were merely out prowling."

The bulky soldier looked utterly astounded. He swallowed several times.

"I do not understand," he mumbled again.

General Vigo made a fierce face at him.

"You are a spy, an employee of the Inca in Gray!" roared the general dictator of Delezon.

Soldiers gripped the prisoner. Sharp points of bayonets pressed against his back. Any attempt at escape would have been suicidal.

"*No, no, mi amigo,*" the prisoner stuttered. "This is not true."

"What!" Fabulously ugly General Vigo waved an arm, shrilled, "Search him!"

They began to strip the prisoner. The coat came off first, then the shirt. A hissing of surprised gasps went up.

"*Caramba!*" General Vigo exploded, eyes bulging. "Such muscles on a man I have never seen before."

They finished stripping the prisoner, and, when they stood back, more than one man was pop-eyed with amazement. They had uncovered a physical giant, with incredible muscles. The officers who had brought the prisoner in shivered a little, and wondered if they had not just had one of the narrow escapes of their lives.

Most striking of all, perhaps, was the remarkable fineness of the prisoner's skin texture and its striking bronze color.

70

General Vigo stared. He worked his thick shoulders inside his coat as if trying to get rid of an invisible weight which had just settled upon them.

"Who," he demanded, "are you, señor?"

"Doc Savage," the prisoner said quietly.

General Vigo had a fit. He jumped up and down. He screamed and beat his own chest with his fists.

"Doc Savage!" he shrieked. "So you are working for the Inca in Gray!"

General Vigo jumped up and down some more, mauled himself, and slavered a little in his rage.

"No!" he howled. "You, Doc Savage, are probably yourself the Inca in Gray!"

DOC SAVAGE had schooled himself to show no emotion unless he so willed. So the fact that his countenance now remained inscrutable did not mean he was unsurprised. He was learning things.

According to previous information, the Inca in Gray had been an affliction peculiar to the republic of Santa Amoza; but here was General Vigo of Delezon flying into a rage over the name of the Inca in Gray. That angle would bear investigation.

"What is the Inca in Gray?" Doc Savage asked.

General Vigo went through the motion of a grotesque jumping jack.

"He is a devil!" he screamed. "He is a fiend, this Inca in Gray! He is a tool of Santa Amoza!"

"Will you be more specific?" Doc requested.

"Some of my leading generals have been murdered, murdered strangely with a weird gray dust on their faces and hands," General Vigo snarled. "There has been other sabotage. And, worst of all, there is the uprising."

"What do you mean?" Doc Savage queried.

"The natives, the uncivilized Indians of the jungle," General Vigo growled. "For generations they have been peaceful and have given no trouble. But lately they have gone on the warpath. They are raiding our villages."

He paused, scowled darkly at Doc Savage.

"It is the work of the Inca in Gray," he continued. "The Inca in Gray is a devil. He has convinced the natives that he is the leader destined to bring back their ancient power and glory."

Doc Savage persisted, "What ancient power and glory?"

"The natives are descendants of the Incas," General Vigo advised. "They have a natural hate of all white men. The Inca in Gray has capitalized on that."

Doc Savage was silent a moment.

"Would it be any use," he queried, "to assure you that my presence here is for the purpose of ferreting out the Inca in Gray—and ascertaining what happened to my aide, Long Tom?"

General Vigo's expression changed slightly. He looked as if he half believed the bronze man.

"Turn on the machine," General Vigo told one of the orderlies. "We will examine this man's clothing."

The orderly went into the next room. In a moment, a weird hum sounded from the chamber.

Doc Savage stood calmly as the clothing he had worn was picked up and carried into the next room. Doc Savage was marched after the clothing. His guards kept their guns ready.

A queer machine stood in the adjacent room, a large box of an affair from which wires ran to a generator on the floor. Both the box and the generator were making the humming noise.

"Guard the door," directed General Vigo. Then the general dictator of Delezon frowned at Doc Savage. "You know what this device is?"

Doc nodded. "Certainly. An ultra-violet ray machine."

"Then you probably guess why I have it?" suggested General Vigo.

Again the bronze man nodded. "The device will bring out hidden messages on cloth, paper and——"

"Enough," grunted Vigo. Then to his orderlies, "Examine the clothing."

They seized the uniform which they had removed from Doc Savage and held it under the black lens of the ultra-violet lantern, a piece at a time. The shirt, the trousers, the blouse, revealed nothing.

Far from looking disappointed, General Vigo seemed a bit relieved.

Under the ultra-violet lens they shoved the undershirt which Doc Savage had taken from the burly soldier he had overpowered back by the wrecked plane.

And on the undershirt appeared a crude map, and row after row of figures.

AN ENRAGED ROAR came from General Vigo. He was plainly surprised; and even Doc Savage, with his great composure, was momentarily moved into a flicker of annoyed astonishment.

Doc Savage knew instantly what had happened. There had been no chance to tamper with his clothing after he had taken it from the burly soldier. Therefore, that soldier had been a spy. Probably there were many of these in Delezon. It had been the bronze man's misfortune to impersonate one of them.

The writing on the undershirt had been done with invisible ink; but few invisible inks are impervious to detection with ultra-violet light. This one certainly was not. When the room was darkened, the writing glowed out distinctly.

General Vigo examined the map. He seemed to swell with rage.

"Our front line!" he snarled. "It shows our gun emplacements, our supply roads, our airports—everything!"

Doc Savage began, "The clothing came from a man whom——"

"Silence!" roared General Vigo.

Doc Savage did not grow silent. He raised his voice, and its thunder beat down the objections of the general dictator of Delezon. The bronze man talked, spoke rapidly, heedless of the bayonets which menaced him at first. And General Vigo, because there was nothing else to do, listened, heard him through.

Doc Savage told the whole story, omitting nothing, beginning with the attempt on his own life in New York, telling the adventure on the dirigible, and ending with an account of exactly what had happened in Santa Amoza. He got several surprising reactions from General Vigo.

"I did not seize Señorita Anita Carcetas!" howled General Vigo. "I do not have to kidnap women to win my wars!"

"But there was a message to minister Serrato, saying that you had the young woman and that she would be executed unless Santa Amoza surrendered," Doc told him.

"It was no message from me, señor!" General Vigo shouted. "Some one else must have sent it. Either that or war minister Serrato lied."

"There are certain indications pointing to minister Serrato as the Inca in Gray," Doc Savage said.

General Vigo was obviously engaged in deep thought. He turned off the ultra-violet lantern, then took several slow turns about the room, hands locked together behind his back.

Suddenly he stopped, cracked an order at his officers.

"Assemble a firing squad," he directed.

Small lights came into the bronze man's flake-gold eyes. "You do not believe me?" he queried.

"I believe you are Doc Savage," said General Vigo.

Doc began, "Then why——"

"Don those clothes," General Vigo snapped.

73

Because there was nothing else to do, Doc Savage obeyed.

Doc Savage, closely guarded, was marched toward a high stockade, the adobe walls of which were perforated along the top for machine gun emplacements. The only door in the wall of this fort was narrow. They headed for it.

Mingling with the crowd of onlookers, making himself inconspicuous, was the small man with the pocked face and the evil grin. Without being too forward about it, he was gathering all the information he could. The pock-faced fellow craned his neck time and again and managed to get several good looks at Doc Savage.

Doc Savage walked with a steady tread, his bronze features showing no slightest sign of fear. He did not argue.

The bronze man was led through the narrow door into the enclosure, the same enclosure into which Long Tom had been escorted some hours previously. Doc was marched to the same bullet-pocked wall against which Long Tom had stood. He was backed against it. The soldiers withdrew.

"A bandage for your eyes?" General Vigo asked bluntly.

"No," Doc Savage said distinctly.

The door through the stockade was closed. The firing squad lined up before their victim.

Outside the stockade, the pock-faced little man with the evil face mingled with the throng. He kept a hand tucked behind an ear, listening intently. He managed to pick up the ominous commands from within. General Vigo was giving the execution orders himself.

"Ready!" roared the general dictator of Delezon.

"Aim——"

"Fire——"

A volley of shot blazed out, frightening pigeons off the roofs of near-by buildings.

In the comparative silence that followed, a strange sound was heard. It was a trilling, small, eerie, fantastic, carrying from within the stockade in amazing fashion. It might have been the song of some exotic feathered thing of the jungle. The trilling was quite distinct at first, but it faded slowly, seeming to go away into nothingness until only the memory of its weird tremolo remained.

The small, pock-faced spectator crept away as soon as he could do so without attracting attention. He went directly to a squalid house in the poorer section and entered. The house, after the South American fashion, had a patio, a tiny court in the center. The dwellings of Delezon had these patios, regardless of how poor they might be.

74

Shortly, a pigeon arose from the patio. The bird attracted no attention, for there were other pigeons in the village, and their resemblance to the carrier breed of bird was close enough to cause confusion.

No one paid much attention to pigeons anyway.

Chapter 11

DISASTER

Doc Savage's stratosphere dirigible hung motionless considerably more than a score of thousands of feet over Alcala, capital city of Santa Amoza.

Monk, the homely chemist, was using the device, which, for lack of a better name, was called the "infra eye." This was simply an elaboration of the portable apparatus which Doc Savage had used in the darkness. It consisted of a projector which sent out light waves of a wave-length invisible to the human eye downward. There was a scanning panel for observation purposes.

Monk had been observing for some time. His small eyes were acquiring a strained squint.

"Wonder what's happened to Doc?" he grumbled. "That fire we saw a few hours ago on the edge of a flying field, I wonder if that could have been something happening to his plane?"

"Our orders were to stick up here until we got some word from Doc," Ham said shortly. "Doc wanted this Inca in Gray, whoever he is, to think the dirigible had been destroyed."

Monk went on with his muttering. "No planes have left Alcala except that crate that looked like an old Jenny. Blazes, I expected some word from Doc before now!"

Monk reached suddenly for a powerful telescope, one of Doc's own design. Then he seized the controls of the airship, manipulated them, and the craft began to descend.

There was a bank of fleecy clouds below. This hid the earth completely as far as inspection with the naked eye was concerned. The infra rays however penetrated the dense cloud bank, which was the reason they had been using the rays.

"What is the idea, you missing link?" Ham demanded.

"I see something," Monk told him. "Shut up."

The ship sank, altimeter needles marching slowly backward. There was almost no sound since the motors were turning over very slowly. They entered the clouds.

"Some one will see us from below," Ham snapped.

"Use your head," Monk retorted. "This bus is camouflaged so you can't hardly see it from below. An' that infra

76

eye ain't so hot when you want to make a detailed inspection. I saw somethin' I'm gonna use this telescope on."

The clouds began to thin out. The ship had penetrated to the under side.

"Hold 'er," grunted Monk.

Ham took the controls and leveled the dirigible out.

Monk opened a floor hatch, lay down beside it, and focused the powerful telescope carefully. He seemed very interested in what he was studying. It was noticeable that the telescope was not pointed directly at Alcala which was almost below, but was slanted off to one side—toward the battle front, in fact.

"Well," Ham snapped, "do I get a look?"

Monk surrendered the telescope reluctantly.

Ham focused the lenses to his own vision.

"Just a plane," he said.

"Yeah, but watch how it's actin'," Monk grunted. "An' notice them little patches of white vapor behind it."

Ham inspected the patches of vapor which had been mentioned. These were very vague, and were some distance behind the plane.

"Smoke from anti-aircraft shells," said the dapper lawyer. "What is queer about that?"

"Just keep watching," Monk advised.

Ham watched. He had not been doing that long when he stiffened.

THE PLANE they were observing was behaving somewhat uncertainly. It did not stay level. Numerous times it slipped. Once it fell off in a short spin before it was hauled out.

"Something wrong with the plane," Ham said.

Monk nodded. "Practically unmanageable. Probably some of its control wires have been shot away."

They continued to watch. It was doubtful if the dirigible could be distinguished with the naked eye from the earth below. Powerful glasses might have revealed it, but even that was a bit doubtful, due to its camouflaging.

Monk leaped to the controls, adjusted them, sent the airship toward the front lines. This enabled Ham to observe the strangely acting plane more distinctly.

Unexpectedly a puff of white smoke came from the tail of the ship. The craft veered, straightened. Another puff of smoke appeared. Then a third.

The plane flew some distance. Then smoke appeared again. This time it came for a longer interval. It stopped. A moment later it resumed.

"Catch on?" Monk grunted.

"Dry up," Ham said. "Watch this."

A few moments later the plane had deposited three balls of smoke in the air, three rather long wads of smoke, then three more balls.

"Continental code," Monk barked. "I can read it with the naked eye now."

"S.O.S." Ham agreed. "It means whoever is down there wants help."

"Think it's Doc?" Monk demanded.

The two men exchanged glances. The usual animosity with which they inspected each other was missing. They seemed to reach a common conclusion without the use of words.

"Down we go," Monk grunted.

The homely chemist lunged to the controls. He wrenched the throttle levers open. The motors blurted out a great howl. He stroked another lever. A scream came from the tail portion of the dirigible. The rocket tubes had been put into operation. The airship began to give an excellent imitation of a bullet as fast as speed was concerned.

Details of the scene below took on distinctness. The earth seemed to swell. The front line trenches became discernible.

The plane, it developed, was farther away than had first appeared. It was, in fact, well within Delezon territory, and would be deeper in Delezon before they overhauled it, for it was flying at a good speed, although its behavior was as erratic as before.

Monk seized the telescope, focused it, stared.

"It's Doc!" he barked.

"How can you tell?" Ham demanded.

"He isn't wearing gloves," Monk explained. "His hands look like bronze."

They began to manipulate the dirigible's controls, shutting off the rocket tubes first. This was necessary in order to decrease the speed of the craft so that it would not overshoot the plane below. They managed this very efficiently. The airship drew alongside the plane, slightly above it, perhaps a hundred yards separating the two aircraft.

Monk used the telescope again, readjusting the lenses for the short distance. What he saw caused him to emit a bark of surprise. He lunged to the rudder wheel of the dirigible, turned it and whipped the airship almost alongside the plane. He stared again.

"That guy ain't Doc!" Monk yelled. "He's got make-up on so he'll look like Doc."

The plane suddenly shed its erratic manner of flight. The

pilot delved into his cockpit and came up with a hand machine gun.

"A trap!" Ham shouted. "Take 'er up!"

MONK HIT the altitude controls of the airship. The big, reinforced alloy metal bag jumped.

Simultaneously, a shattering roar came from the side of the control cabin, a sound as of many drumsticks beating very hard. They looked at the windows. These were becoming cobwebbed with cracks. The glass was bullet-proof, and obviously machine-gun lead was crashing into it.

Shadows of an attacking air squadron swept over them like a dark cloud. The ships zoomed, circled and came back again. Their machine guns were winking red eyes on the cowl. There were half a dozen of these ships, and not one of them bore a marking to designate it as belonging to the military force of either Delezon or Santa Amoza.

Their lead made a great drumming and roaring on the dirigible. It was not, however, doing a great deal of damage. The control cabin was proof against anything less than a field gun shell. The gas bags, the dirigible's skin, of course, could not be made bullet-proof, due to the necessity for lightness. But puncturing the bags would do no great damage. For the gas cells were coated inside with a spongy substance which expanded and closed all but the largest of apertures.

Monk had the altitude control lever far back. The ship was all but standing on its tail. He jerked other levers. The rocket tubes began to make moaning sounds.

"They ain't gonna faze us," Monk grunted.

Ham nodded and snapped, "Notice the lack of markings on the ships. They must be followers of this mysterious Inca in Gray."

"Whoever he is, that Inca in Gray ain't no piker," Monk mumbled. "He does things on a big scale."

The dirigible was beginning to leap upward in the sky.

There was a moan off to one side as an attacking plane came down, then hauled up swiftly. A small bomb detached from its under side, and came boring for the dirigible.

"Watch it," Ham yelled.

Monk wrenched the controls. The big dirigible, for all of its terrific speed, veered abruptly. The bomb—it must have weighed in excess of a hundred pounds—missed them, and hurtled down to dig a great pit in the jungle below, well behind the war front of Delezon.

Monk peered downward at the pit the explosive had

made, mentally visualizing what would have happened if it had struck them. It was not a pleasant mind picture.

Suddenly Ham was screaming again. "Drop 'er! Drop 'er!"

Monk looked up, too late. One of the planes was rushing toward them. It was almost upon them. The pilot was out of the cockpit, hanging on with one hand, using the other hand to handle the stick and guide his ship.

He was going to crash them, ram them deliberately with his own plane. It was a desperate expedient, and probably the only one which would insure success under the circumstances.

At the last possible moment, the enemy pilot pitched clear of his plane. He was a cunning fellow. He held his body so that the very force of the air and his momentum caused him to hurtle downward under the dirigible.

The plane hit the gas bag squarely. It buried itself almost completely in the cellular structure of gas compartments and girders. The concussion was terrific. Flame burst from the plane, which had been turned into a missile. This fire, however, was almost instantly snuffed out, for the gas which furnished buoyancy to the airship was not only non-inflammable itself, but was effective as fire extinguishing vapor in smothering flames.

Both Monk and Ham were stunned by the impact.

SHOCKS HAVE rather a strange effect upon the human system. A shock will produce unconsciousness, while another and similar shock, perhaps of lesser violence, will, under the proper combination of circumstances, have the effect of returning that consciousness. It was thus with the crash as the dirigible struck.

Not all of the ship's buoyancy had been lost. So that it did not fall very hard. The jungle cushioned its landing also, and the stout metal framework of the control room preserved Monk and Ham. A loud hissing came from the ruptured pipes of the mechanism which conditioned air.

Monk's sturdier constitution caused him to come to his feet first. He listened. The planes were moaning about overhead.

Came a jarring explosion. Fifty yards distant, earth and tree fragments spouted upward. The earth gave a distinct jerk. It was a bomb dropped by one of the planes above.

Ham was sitting up. There was in his eyes that unclearness which indicated he still did not fully comprehend what was occurring.

"Ham!" Monk shouted, then slapped the dapper lawyer's face.

Ham growled, "I'll skin you alive for that," and came to his feet.

"Run for it!" Monk barked. "They're laying eggs on us!"

The homely chemist opened the hatchway and stumbled out into the thick jungle growth, closely followed by his more slender companion. Staccato rattle of machine guns sounded overhead, and bullets pattered in the brush about them. They ran.

A squealing grunt from behind brought Monk up short.

"Habeas!" he cried, and turned.

"Forget the hog!" Ham barked.

That suggestion was proof that Ham had almost completely recovered himself.

Monk shoved out a foot, upset Ham ignominiously in the brush, and yelled, "That hog is worth six lawyers!"

The homely chemist plunged back through the undergrowth toward the stricken ship, heedless of danger from bombs and machine-gun bullets. His long, apelike arms stretched ahead of him to part the dense jungle creepers.

Ham got up from where he had fallen when Monk tripped him, scowled darkly, then followed the homely chemist. He drew near the dirigible wreck in time to see Monk disappear into the hatchway.

Almost simultaneously, a squad of men in clothing almost unbelievably dirty and bedraggled burst into view and ran for the fallen dirigible.

"Monk!" Ham shrieked. "Watch out!"

The men, it appeared, were armed. They lifted rifles. These whacked. A storm of bullets drove Ham into cover.

Inside the dirigible, Monk was bawling angrily. He burst out of the wreckage, carrying the pig, Habeas Corpus, by one saillike ear. It could not be said that Monk gave Habeas the gentlest of treatment. The instant the homely chemist saw the armed men, he hurled the pig through the air into the nearest clump of brush.

Then Monk doubled around the dirigible wreckage in a frantic effort to escape.

"Run!" Ham bawled encouragement.

Then Ham suddenly discovered that he had more to do than vocally encourage Monk. There were more of the strangely shabby men in the jungle. They were creeping up on him. They were, in fact, only a few yards distant. Now they rushed.

Ham was no unskilled fighter. Particularly was he adept at use of his sword cane, but that had been left behind in the excitement. It was somewhere in the ruined airship. Ham struck out furiously with his fists.

But he was fighting men who were not afraid, and who had some ability. They swarmed over him. He was hopelessly outnumbered and beaten down, tripped, held.

"Monk!" Ham shrieked again. "Run for it! I'm all right!"

There was a crashing and thumping and struggling in the brush near by, and after that had continued a while it approached. A swarm of men were bringing a captive.

The prisoner was Monk.

He looked at Ham and growled, "So you're all right. What a liar!"

In the brush, Habeas Corpus grunted anxiously.

"Ah, a peeg," one of the dirty, disheveled men murmured in bad English. "We shall have fresh meat."

Two or three of the men were deployed. There was brief, tumultuous struggle, followed by several startled squeals.

"Got heem," said a voice.

THE MAN who seemed to be in charge of the party approached them, looked them over. The fellow's face was not a nice thing to examine. He smirked evilly at them.

Then the fellow walked a few yards away into an opening in the jungle, and, with his arms, made signals to the planes which still buzzed about overhead. The pilots of the ships observed, waved back. After that the aircraft moaned away over the jungle and their sound was soon lost to hearing.

The leader of the jungle party came and stared down at Monk and Ham. He jerked his head in the direction taken by the departing planes.

"They will bear good news to our master, The Inca in Gray," he said.

Somebody in the back of the group laughed, spoke in Spanish.

"And they will return bearing even better news, let us hope," this man said.

"*Si, si,*" the first man agreed. "The Inca in Gray is striking fast now. It will not be long until his plans are completed and his ends are gained."

Monk, who could speak Spanish, put in, "And what end is this Inca in Gray after?"

The homely chemist received a resounding kick for his temerity in putting the question. Eyes pain blurred, Monk looked at Ham. The glance the dapper lawyer returned did not hold much sympathy.

The captors now began to hold a consultation. They spoke loudly, frankly, and as they did so, they watched their prisoners as if enjoying the reaction which the words produced.

82

"Would it be better to kill them now?" one ruminated. "Or should we receive orders from the master, the Inca in Gray."

"Now," a man voted.

"No, no," said another.

"Why not?" demanded the first. "They are our enemies. Death to such."

"I know," said the first, "but the Inca in Gray prefers to know all and to direct all moves. It is to our advantage to receive instructions. The prisoners will be killed anyway, of course."

"That is as it should be," said another. "They are followers of that bronze man, Doc Savage."

The man who said this spoke the words somewhat nervously, much as one might mention a very real personal devil. This caused some of the others to chuckle mirthfully.

"Our brother has the heart of a flower," they laughed. "He fears a dead man."

"I do not," insisted the other.

"Doc Savage is dead," he was reminded. "And you fear him."

Chapter 12

THE HUMORIST

Doc Savage's death, to paraphrase the statement attributed to a famous man of letters, was somewhat exaggerated.

Doc Savage was in a room which was not merely dark. It was black—black with an intensity that seemed to deny the possibility of any light existing anywhere. This darkness was the more noteworthy, because somewhere outside there should be brilliant tropical sunlight.

The bronze man was in a dungeon somewhere under the compound's walls. He had been there some time. Long Tom Roberts was in the dungeon with him.

Long Tom was talking, had been talking in exactly the same tone and repeating many of the same words for some time. Long Tom was not a man who indulged in profanity. He was using no swear words, but he managed to put into his monotonous voice a good deal of gripping vituperation.

Long Tom had ridded himself of opinions concerning the hot weather, Santa Amoza, Delezon, General Vigo, the Inca in Gray, South America in general, and had now gotten around to those gentlemen who are frequently blamed for wars.

"Munitions makers," Long Tom intoned, "they suck the blood from nations . . . . murderers of the masses . . . . they've got me here . . . . fiends . . . ."

It was strange talk for Long Tom. It was exactly such conversation, in fact, as might be attributed to an insane man. There was a madness in the tone, too. The guards outside, hearing the interminable condemnation exchanged knowing glances. They had heard men go mad before in these dungeons. It did not, however, usually happen so soon.

However, a close listener might have detected another sound which was almost drowned by Long Tom's interminable talking. This was a series of low whizzings. These tiny noises kept up steadily. The guards outside were not close enough to hear them.

Long Tom finished with munitions makers and went back to the Inca in Gray for conversational matter.

"Infernal devil," the pallid electrical wizard mumbled,

"killing people . . . . no visible reason . . . . something big must be behind him. . . ."

A guard pacing outside shivered. The air down here was stifling for want of ventilation. The guard tried to smoke a cigarette, but it stuck to his lips. He felt thirsty.

The dull monotone of Long Tom's incantation went on and on, sentences disjointed, thoughts half phrased. Under it, the small mysterious scraping and buzzing continued.

The buzzing was inside the dungeon. Suddenly a tiny pin point of light appeared. This grew to an irregular slit, but very slowly. Minutes were required for the phenomena. The slit lengthened, changed direction. It assumed the shape of a "U" lying on its side.

The lock was being cut out of the heavy door.

Doc Savage spoke in a low voice.

"It is ready," he said simply.

Long Tom ceased his mumbling.

"Whe-ew," he said in a perfectly normal voice. "It's about time. I was running out of things to talk about."

LONG TRAINING had put an incredible power in Doc Savage's fingers. The cracks in the door which afforded his only grip were not large, but, employing them, he managed to swing the heavy portal inward.

Dim light from outside filtered into the room. Falling across the floor, this luminance disclosed the ingenious drill which the bronze man had fashioned from two belt buckles —his own and Long Tom's. A piece of wood, ripped from a bench, provided a handle. Long Tom's interminable conversation had been to cover the sound the drill was making as it cut around the lock.

"Come," said Doc Savage. "But be careful about the noise."

"I know," Long Tom breathed. "The guard."

With a stealth and lack of noise that a tomcat would have envied, the bronze man stalked along the dim passages. He could see the sentry shortly. The fellow had gone to a water bucket, which stood on the passage floor, and was drinking. He was taking the water noisily as some diners take their soup.

There was no noise, no struggle of consequence, after Doc Savage seized the man. Bronze fingers simply found nerve centers on the back of the fellow's neck, squeezed, and the man became unconscious. Doc laid him gently on the ground.

Closely trailed by Long Tom, the bronze man worked upward. The inside of the stockade wall, which looked so thick, was hollow, in part, being honey-combed by stair-ways, passages, and small rooms. These afforded them a method of reaching the top.

They came out through a small door upon the runway which ran around the inside of the stockade. A single good leap would put them atop the stockade. Doc Savage made it. He extended a helping hand to Long Tom, for it was quite a jump.

They did not kill time. The drop below them was not a thing to be taken casually. One thing was in their favor, however. The stockade wall was not vertical by any manner of means. It sloped outward, and, although it could hardly be climbed from below, one might slide down it and friction would somewhat delay the descent.

"Let me tackle it first," Doc Savage said. "And be careful."

Without perceptible hesitation, the bronze man stepped over the edge of the wall. There was loud whizzing sound as he went down. This attracted the attention of a soldier across the street. The fellow stopped and stared, mouth open. Apparently, it did not occur to him to shout, or to unsling the rifle which he carried across his back.

The shock absorbing qualities of tremendous leg muscles came into valuable play as the bronze man hit the packed ground at the foot of the stockade wall. He did not try to remain upright, for that would have been impossible. He let himself go down, almost flat, but he was up again instantly.

"Now," he called to Long Tom.

Long Tom patently did not like what was ahead of him. He made a fierce face, sucked in a full breath, and stepped off the edge. He had used the best judgment. Friction burned him through his clothing. His skin was blistered in several places.

The next instant he was on the ground. Doc Savage had caught him, cushioned in part the shock of his landing.

They ran.

Across the street, the soldier came to life; he emitted a howl that would have done credit to an Andes jaguar. He fought to get the gun off his back.

Doc and Long Tom leaped toward him. They reached the fellow before his rifle came into use. They fell upon him. Doc used his fists and the man was abruptly silent.

There was doorway near by, open. They dived into this, carrying the soldier. The room was empty. They left the soldier.

A door took them into a patio from which they climbed onto a roof, and eventually reached the next street. It was the hot part of the day, the siesta hour. Even the war could not break the habits of the Delezonians. Most of the soldiers were having their hour or two of slumber.

"Where now?" Long Tom demanded.

"This way," Doc Savage said. "We have a job to do."

AROUND THE headquarters of General Vigo there was quiet. A single sentry paced patrol, and his manner was drowsy. He stopped frequently to perch on the veranda rail and smoke.

There were bushes immediately below the veranda rail. The sentry sighed and drew deeply on his cigarette.

The next instant he was off the rail. He made almost no sound. The bushes fluttered only slightly as he disappeared into them, drawn by a pair of corded bronze arms.

For some moments Doc Savage worked on the nerve centers at the back of the fellow's neck. The sentry became limp, and seemingly slept. Smoke, which he had drawn out of a cigarette, curled slowly from his lips and nostrils.

Long Tom whispered, "That was nice."

"Wait here," Doc Savage breathed back.

The bronze man made a cautious survey. No one was in sight. The shouting of the soldier who had observed their escape from the compound had failed to attract attention. Two things could explain this. The Delezonians were a people who naturally did a great deal of shouting over trivial things. There was also some drinking among soldiers back from the front on leave.

Doc Savage eased over the veranda rail.

The windows of General Vigo's quarters were open. Gliding to them, Doc noted the layout of the room. The door to the corridor was next to, and at right angles to one of the windows. The bronze man went to this window. He eased through, crossed the room, and caught sight of his quarry.

General Vigo was alone, leaning over a map into which he was sticking colored pins. He chanced to be standing so that he was almost certain to observe Doc Savage as the bronze man entered, and he gave no sign of intending to move.

Doc Savage had no intention of waiting until General Vigo decided to shift his position. The unconscious sentry might be discovered at any moment, or they might find that he and Long Tom had escaped from the stockade dungeon. The bronze man flexed the muscles of his throat in peculiar fashion.

"General Vigo," he called in Spanish. His voice was

different, meek and mild as if it were a common soldier speaking. "Come quickly, I wish to show you something."

Now, remarkably enough, these words did not seem to come from Doc Savage, but from the other side of the room in which General Vigo stood. Doc was using ventriloquism. General Vigo faced the spot from which the words had appeared to emanate. A door was there.

Seeing no one, General Vigo snapped, "What is it? Who wants——"

His voice was abruptly choked off by corded bronze fingers which had clamped upon his throat. General Vigo was no weakling. He struggled violently, kicking backward, driving his fists. Doc Savage received two terrific blows. He kept his throat grip.

The bronze man hit General Vigo, not as heavily as he intended, on the jaw. Vigo only struggled more violently. Doc tried again with his fist. Fist and jaw, meeting, made a sound as of two hardwood blocks colliding violently.

WHEN GENERAL VIGO awakened to sit up and rub his jaw and make numerous ugly grimaces, there was scrawny brush about him. He listened. He could hear plane motors, and, straining his neck, could see indistinctly a number of his own military airplane hangars. He was, he decided, near the airport on the outskirts of his headquarters village.

General Vigo looked at Doc Savage. The bronze man stood near by. His metallic features were expressionless. Long Tom was on the opposite side.

General Vigo looked as if he wanted to swear. Instead, he grinned.

"It is not healthy to kidnap the general dictator of a country the size of Delezon," he said.

Doc Savage began speaking.

"Why did you fake those executions?" the bronze man asked.

"What executions?" General Vigo demanded.

"Those of Long Tom and myself," the bronze man elaborated. "You stood me against that wall, and, in a very loud voice, gave the order for the firing squad to shoot. They fired into the wall, but far to one side of where I stood. Long Tom says you did exactly the same thing in his case."

"For which you owe me thanks," General Vigo grunted.

"And for which you owe us an explanation," Doc Savage told him.

General Vigo shrugged. "The reason is simple."

"Suppose you explain it," Doc told him.

"I desire the end of the Inca in Gray," General Vigo snapped. "I would not hesitate to shoot the devil. But I did not want to execute innocent men. I do not believe in executions. Therefore, I arranged the fake shooting. The men in the firing squad can be trusted. Word would be spread that you were dead. To all intents and purposes, you *would* be dead."

"Which would get you what?" Doc queried.

"If the Inca in Gray suddenly dropped out of sight, after, for instance, I had pulled my little execution trick on you, that would be suspicious, eh?" General Vigo demanded.

"So that was the reason," Doc said.

"It was," the general dictator of Delezon growled. "And now, suppose you let me go, señor."

Doc Savage shook a slow negative. Then he stared steadily at General Vigo.

The bronze man's eyes were capable of doing strange things. Nature had given them an unusual appearance; but long practice had given them a good deal more power, had enabled them to express things. The flake-gold eyes had almost as much ability to express emotion as had the face of an experienced actor. The bronze man's eyes were grim now, and utterly threatening.

General Vigo squirmed uneasily.

"Dios mio," he mumbled hoarsely. "I believe you intend to kill me."

That was exactly the impression Doc Savage had been trying to create.

"You have," the bronze man said, "one chance to live."

"What is it?" growled General Vigo, somewhat weakly.

"Do as you are told," he was advised.

General Vigo swallowed several times. He said nothing.

Then Doc Savage did a totally unexpected thing. He drew from his clothing a heavy automatic military pistol and extended it to General Vigo. The latter took it, and looked stunned.

General Vigo would not have admitted it himself, but he was scared. Just how frightened he was, how thoroughly cowed, was evident from his action now. He held the gun in his hand, but made no attempt to use it.

"The weapon is not loaded," Doc Savage said. "You will walk behind us, pointing the gun at us as if we were your prisoners. We will walk on to the airport. You will ask for your special plane; presumably, you have one, have you not?"

General Vigo nodded. He was watching the bronze man's

eyes. That was a mistake, but the general dictator of Delezon had no way of knowing that he was subjecting himself
to what was literally a hypnotic spell.

"I have a private plane," he admitted.

"Walk," Doc Savage directed.

General Vigo got up. Doc Savage and Ham strode a
little ahead of him, one to the right and one to the left,
maintaining such a position that they could watch the man
behind them.

They marched out on the tarmac of the Delezon military
airport.

SENTRIES CHALLENGED the moment they were in view.
General Vigo gave what was evidently the password for
the day, and he added for good measure, "These men are my
prisoners."

The sentries passed them.

They approached the hangars. Their presence was observed, and officers came out, lined up, saluted. The com-
mandant of the field advanced.

"My private plane," General Vigo told him. "Get it
ready for the air at once. I will fly it myself."

The officer looked dumfounded, saluted, said, "But you
cannot fly, general *mio*."

General Vigo got himself out of that very nicely. He
put his ugly face out and growled, "Do not question my
orders. I will show you whether or not I can fly."

General Vigo's plane was a five-place cabin ship, an
American job, modern, fast, new. A single twist of the
propeller started the motor roaring. Long Tom and Doc
Savage climbed into the cabin.

There were two bucket seats for pilots forward. Doc
Savage took one of these. Controls were before both. General Vigo got into the other bucket.

"Good work," Doc Savage told him.

General Vigo scowled, looking very much as if he had
just eaten a full meal of green apples. He stuck his un-
lovely visage out of the plane window and bawled an order.
The chocks were pulled.

General Vigo grasped the control wheel; but Doc Savage
did the flying. The motor bawled. The plane ran across the
field, picked up its tail, and jumped.

Doc Savage headed the ship for Alcala, capital city of
Santa Amoza. The motor droned steadily. It was a good
motor with plenty of power to spare. Long Tom, back in
the cabin, kept silent, but watched the jungle and desert
below.

"See if you can find binoculars," Doc Savage called from the controls.

Long Tom searched, probing through door pockets, and in little compartments above the seats.

"You will find them toward the rear," General Vigo shouted gruffly.

Long Tom looked, located the binoculars, and passed them to Doc Savage. There was a glass hatch immediately above the control cockpit. This was grease-smeared from the motor. Doc Savage opened it for clearer vision and focused the binoculars at the sky. There had been clouds earlier in the day, but these had dispersed. The heavens were an inverted bowl of white and heat.

The bronze man evidently did not find what he was looking for. He passed the binoculars back to Long Tom.

"Keep an eye open for the stratosphere dirigible," he suggested.

Long Tom nodded and worked with the fastening which secured the cabin windows. He did not have his window open when Doc Savage's voice came again, a grim crash.

"Never mind," the bronze man said.

Something about the words, or perhaps it was the sudden grimness in the bronze man's voice, caused Long Tom to spin and stare. Doc Savage was looking at something ahead, to one side, on the earth. Long Tom followed the bronze man's glance.

It was the dirigible—the wreckage of it, rather. Doc Savage banked the plane sharply, sent it toward the crash scene.

The dirigible now looked like nothing so much as a silver egg which dropped urgently in the jungle. The egg aspect, however, did not persist for long. The true size of the stratosphere craft became apparent as they drew closer. Then, too, they could see that the aërial vessel had hit with a great deal of force.

Doc Savage put the plane very low. Wind from the propeller stirred the jungle leaves as they hurtled along. It was obviously his intention to examine the dirigible as closely as possible.

They flew past the airship.

Long Tom spoke in a voice that might have come from Death himself.

"No sign of them," he said. "They must have been crushed in the cabin."

Doc Savage banked the plane, went past again. Their second scrutiny was no more availing than the first. Nor did a third show them a sign of life. Doc Savage backed on the stick and the ship took a little altitude. They looked for a spot that would do for a landing.

The jungle ran for miles. Clearings were scarce, small; but there were a few. The nearest was at least two miles distant.

The clearing, when they reached it, caused Long Tom to shake his head. It was smooth enough, but it was terribly small. Doc Savage sent the plane for it. Long Tom shuddered. They would not make it, even with the bronze man's magnificent flying skill.

But they did make it. The craft jerked into what seemed a certain stall just at the edge of the clearing, coasted out of that, went into a slip, straightened, then, miraculously, seemed to have almost no momentum when it landed.

Long Tom got out and looked around and his neck got red. They had something near two hundred feet to spare.

"Long Tom," Doc Savage said, "want to watch the plane?"

Long Tom knew the answer that was expected to that one.

"Sure," he said.

"Take it into the air at the first sign of an attack," Doc Savage directed.

"Sure," said Long Tom. The heartiness in his own voice surprised him. He did not feel it. In fact, he was quite sure that he could never fly a plane out of that small clearing.

Doc Savage seated General Vigo in the plane in one of the wicker seats, and lashed him there. He made the tying a secure job.

"Merely to avoid any complications," the bronze man said.

Doc Savage moved to the jungle, disappeared. The growth was very dense, hot, full of insects. The bronze man took to the trees, the upper boughs of which interlaced to a large extent. He traveled now in a fashion somewhat amazing.

His agile climbing, his breath-taking swings from one bough to another, the long drop through space from one bough to another, were hardly exceeded by a swarm of jungle monkeys which he passed within a few minutes. The monkeys, chattering excitedly, followed him for some little distance, made great uproar.

An individual with less knowledge of animal nature would have thrown sticks at the little beasts, with the result that they would have been excited even more. Doc Savage simply put on speed, hurtling from one tree to another, running along swaying boughs with the ease of a tight-rope walker. He had removed his shoes. His feet, his toes, it might have been noticed, were possessed of a remarkable prehensility

92

which adapted them somewhat to the unusual mode of travel. He left the monkeys behind.

He reached the dirigible.

Some twenty minutes he searched the wreck and its vicinity. He found footprints, plenty of them. Scores of men, most of them barefooted had swarmed around the ship. The bronze man found empty machine gun shells, but, since these frequently lay where there were no human tracks, he knew that they must have been dumped from grabsacks attached to airplane machine guns.

Monk and Ham's trail he finally found. He traced it out. He came to the spot where they had been captured; and there he found ominous signs.

There were scarlet stains on the trampled leaves, leakage from human bodies obviously. There were two indentations where forms had fallen. Doc studied these. They about fitted the statures of Monk and Ham.

BEFORE CONTINUING his hunt, the bronze man removed from the dirigible lockers a small metal case equipped with carrying straps. He carried this and continued his search. Tracks lead away from the spot, footprints in profusion. He studied these closely. Nowhere did he find a print which could be identified as belonging to Monk or Ham. He would have recognized these had they been there. For the bronze man retained in his remarkable memory accurate knowledge of the sizes of footprints made by all of his men.

He lost the trail. The fact that he did was no reflection on his ability at following spoor. The footprints joined unexpectedly a jungle trail which seemed to be a route much in use by soldiers and light artillery in going to and from the front lines.

A good deal of traffic had used the trail recently. A squad of cavalry came up while Doc Savage searched, and the bronze man withdrew to cover to let the Delezonians pass. When they had gone, he continued his hunt.

It was hopeless. The party which had captured Monk and Ham and might be carrying their bodies must have gone in one direction or the other, but it was impossible to tell which. Their footprints had been blotted out completely.

Doc Savage returned to the spot where he had left Long Tom, General Vigo and the plane. Nothing had happened there. Doc took the controls while Long Tom untied General Vigo. The ship taxied to the edge of the clearing, came about with one wheel braked, and stood there with both wheels braked while the motor revved up. With the wheelbrakes released, the craft was off like a shot. It took only a few leaves off the trees as it got out of the clearing.

Doc Savage flew directly to the trail, followed it toward the rear for several miles. He saw marching soldiers, artillery, more cavalry. He flew low and inspected them. No sign of Monk or Ham.

The bronze man flew back toward the front, still hunting, but with equal futility. He flew very low, but the plane was not shot at.

"Was the capture of Monk and Ham reported to you?" Doc asked General Vigo.

"No!" snapped General Vigo. He sounded too angry to be lying.

Doc Savage lifted the plane, headed it toward the front and the republic of Santa Amoza, which lay beyond.

Ugly General Vigo looked curious and uneasy.

"What crazy things are you going to do now?" he demanded.

"We are going to try to promote a merger," Doc Savage told him.

"Merger?" The general dictator of Delezon scowled. "Talk sense, señor."

"Santa Amoza and Delezon have a common enemy," Doc Savage told him.

"I still do not understand, *amigo*," Vigo growled.

"The Inca in Gray," Doc Savage said.

General Vigo blinked, wet his lips. He understood.

"*Si, si*," he said slowly. "But I do not understand this merger talk."

"Think," Doc Savage directed him. "Take everything into consideration. The Inca in Gray has been harassing you. If you will analyze the crimes of this mysterious master mind, you will find that they have come at such times as it seemed you were on the point of whipping Santa Amoza. Is that true?"

General Vigo thought briefly. "It is. *Caramba!* It is."

"Exactly the same thing has happened in Santa Amoza," Doc continued. "The Inca in Gray has been keeping this war going."

General Vigo performed a typical American gesture. He scratched his head.

"This thing, señor, she is just a bit too incredible to believe," he mumbled.

"The Inca in Gray has a tremendous organization," Doc Savage said. "This is no small thing. Whatever the Inca in Gray is after, it is big and undoubtedly will affect the lives of many people."

94

General Vigo nodded, then barked, "What about that merger?"

Doc Savage did not answer. He sent the plane toward Santa Amoza.

Chapter 13

CHEMISTRY

A SMALL BUT RATHER important thing happened in the jungle some miles from the wrecked dirigible after Doc Savage had taken his plane out of sight. A pigeon arose. It did not behave as an ordinary wild pigeon would have. It flew in circles until it had attained a considerable height. Then it lined out—flew straight for Santa Amoza and its capital city, Alcala.

One who knew carrier pigeons would have recognized this bird, from its actions, as belonging to that type.

Monk and Ham had watched the bird released. Both Monk and Ham were very much alive, although somewhat battered. They had been beaten, but they had not been entirely on the receiving end of the punishment, it was evident from the battered countenances of several of their captors. Some of these had noses which had been recently bloodied. It was, as a matter of fact, the drippings from these proboscides which Doc Savage had found.

"They tied a note to that pigeon," Monk growled. "Wonder what it was?"

"How would I know?" Ham demanded sourly. "Did you notice them showing it to me?"

The two prisoners fell silent, listening. Four guards were with them. All the rest of the party had departed, the departure being coincident with the appearance of a plane which had cruised back and forth a few minutes ago.

Monk and Ham, having been under the mat of the jungle, had not seen the plane, hence had no way of knowing Doc Savage had been in the craft. Nor did they have the slightest inkling that the decreased number of their captors meant that some of them had dashed off madly in an attempt to apprehend the bronze man as he examined the dirigible. Thickness of the jungle had thwarted this attempt, the expeditionary force not even getting close enough for Doc Savage to become aware of their presence.

Monk listened to the grunting of his pig, Habeas Corpus. The shote was tied to a tree in the near-by jungle.

His tether was a wire. It was rather long, and Habeas, by moving to the end of it, could stand a few feet within the tiny clearing where Monk and Ham were being held.

The shote appeared now, stood looking at his master, Monk, big ears distended.

Probably that was what gave Monk his big idea. The homely chemist rolled over on his side, spoke in a low voice to Ham. He used Mayan, a language which very few people outside Doc Savage and his five aides understood.

"Get ready for some fireworks," was the gist of what Monk said in Mayan.

Ham glared as if Monk had just told him they were going to poison somebody, but that was only Ham's manner. He made it a point never to be polite to Monk.

Monk faced Habeas Corpus.

"Señores," said the pig in Spanish. "I object to this treatment."

Nature has neglected to give pigs human voices, so it was manifestly impossible that Habeas did the speaking; but it certainly sounded as if the speech was coming from the porker.

The guards were dumfounded. One even dropped his rifle.

"Si, si, amigos," Habeas continued. "For an ordinary hog this sort of treatment might be in order; but for one of my undeniable abilities——"

It was Monk, of course, throwing his voice. The homely chemist had long ago learned ventriloquism from Doc Savage.

The byplay might have been ridiculous, comical under other circumstances, but here in the jungle, coming in the surprising manner which it did, falling upon the ears of men who were probably superstitious to start with, it had its effect.

It gave Monk and Ham a chance to heave unnoticed to their feet.

MONK AND HAM were both bound, ankle and wrist; that, by no means, meant they were incapable of movement. They could manage quite respectable leaps, and they did so.

Monk howled as he jumped. His war whoop was one that might have been made by a dozen men. Monk always liked his fights noisy. He crashed his bound hands down on the neck of a guard. The fellow collapsed.

Ham took a second guard in the same fashion, striking the fellow near the base of the skull. Two of the captors were left. Monk took one, his tremendous strength working to great advantage. Ham got the last man down. The fellow was no easy victim. He knew something of wrestling. He closed with Ham and began to do painful things to the dapper lawyer's slender frame. Ham twisted frantically, doubled, and suddenly managed to get the man's head between his knees. That was perfect. Ham's bound ankles made it unnecessary to hook his toes for leverage. He squeezed. The victim's tongue began to come out.

Monk and Ham got to their feet almost together and Monk grinned from ear to ear.

"You gotta admit that hog has his uses," he said.

Ham sniffed. Rather than give praise to Habeas, he kept silent. Monk went over and untied the wire from around the neck of Habeas Corpus.

"Let's see how you can run, hog," the homely chemist grunted.

They started to run through the jungle. They ran without the slightest attention to direction, giving all of their attention to keeping the noise down, making speed. After perhaps a mile of that, they devoted another half hour to wiping out their trail. They did this by crawling through the matted tree tops, by wading in a small stream which they found, and by stepping where footprints would not remain. They did this very assiduously, having had their fill of being prisoners. They did not want their late captors to overhaul them.

Came the inevitable time, however, when they had to decide where they were to go.

"Santa Amoza," Ham said.

They agreed on that. At least, Monk did not object.

They looked at the sun. The solar orb was just enough off center to cause some doubt as what might be south, the direction in which Santa Amoza lay.

Monk leveled an arm, said, "That way."

"Wrong," Ham objected. "It's this way."

Ham pointed in a direction almost opposite from that indicated by Monk.

"You're crazy, you shyster," Monk accused. "Weren't you ever a Boy Scout? Can'tcha tell directions?"

They proceeded to express audibly and quite vehemently various unflattering opinions of each other's abilities as jungle guides. Neither was willing to admit the slightest chance that the other might be right, which would not have surprised any one who knew them.

"A weak mind goes with a strong back," Ham told the huge, apish Monk finally. "I am going my own way."

"Go your own way, you animated law book," Monk muttered. "I'm goin' where I know Santa Amoza is."

Without a backward glance, Monk plunged ahead in the direction he had chosen. Habeas Corpus, the pig, grunted unhappily, eyed Ham with what seemed to be an air of expectance, then arose and trotted after Monk, waving his oversize ears at the pestering flies.

Ham, although he would never have admitted it, was nonplused.

SOUNDS OF MONK'S progress ceased. The jungle became silent, and its silence was not pleasant. Ham, in the course of a few minutes, fell to glancing about nervously, experiencing that not uncommon feeling that he was being watched by unseen eyes. His lips tightened. This was no country for one man to tackle alone. Neither himself or Monk.

Ham reached a decision. It hurt him, but he arose and grudgingly turned his steps in the direction taken by Monk. There was a faint trail left by the chemist and his redoubtable pig.

Ham was very alert. There was no sound about him; but the impression he was being followed grew. Great jungle trees overhead created an artificial twilight, and in the dimness objects were difficult to discern with clarity. Ham stopped repeatedly to listen.

He heard a crashing ahead.

"Monk," Ham opened his mouth to call, but closed it grimly. Jungle terror or no jungle terror, he intended to have some fun with Monk. He would devil the apish fellow, make him think he was being attacked.

Ham crowded on as noiselessly and as rapidly as possible. He peered ahead intently, and soon he was rewarded.

Through the trees he could see stooped massive figures moving along the ground, pushing creepers and jungle vegetation aside with long, hairy arms. The light was very indistinct; but that stooped, apelike stride was unmistakable.

Ham's smile spread. He picked up a rock, scuttled forward into a thicket in which the apish form had vanished, drew back his arm and hurled the rock. It smashed into the brush.

The rock smacked through the leaves. It hit something—undoubtedly flesh—with a thump that to Ham was a wholly satisfying sound.

Ham expected to hear a prompt howl from Monk. He was disappointed. There came a high shriek, a great crashing of brush. The noise came in Ham's direction, and Ham's eyes all but fell out. He looked at what came out of growth.

It was a monkey. But such a monkey.

It was larger than a chimpanzee, but smaller than a gorilla. It had no tail and its hair was rust colored.

Strangest of all was the astounding resemblance which the newcomer bore to Monk.

The strange anthropoid advanced toward Ham, making small mumbling sounds which were very like those Monk made on the occasion when he talked to himself.

"Scat!" Ham gasped, and retreated. He promptly had a bit of bad luck. His heel caught in a root and he fell.

The simian marvel bounded toward Ham.

"Scat, drat you!" Ham exploded.

Ham was frankly scared as the creature sprang upon him, but his fright evaporated suddenly as the big simian flung its arms around him and clung there, whimpering, scared.

Ham looked intently into the visage of his new friend. He could not help laughing.

"Monk's twin brother or I hope to kiss that pig Habeas," he gulped.

The simian chattered amiably and Ham got to his feet. The chattering made considerable noise.

"Go away," Ham directed. "One creature looking like you around me is enough. Monk will not want any competition."

The tailless anthropoid bounded up and down—a thing Monk did when he was mad—and gave no indication of holding any thoughts of departure.

Ham scratched his head and ruminated aloud, "I wonder how you tell one of these things to beat it."

The simian made amiable chattering noises.

"Scat," Ham directed. "Shoo. Sooey. Beat it. Vamoose. Go along chop chop."

None of this had any effect. Ham tried clucking as he were driving a horse. That did not work either.

Ham gave it up and fell to studying the creature. He was struck once more by the uncanny resemblance which this jungle dweller bore to the homely chemist, Monk.

At that point came an interruption. Accompanied by a faint noise of shuffling leaves and shifting weeds, the pig Habeas Corpus appeared. The shote caught sight of the anthropoid. Habeas promptly stopped. His big ears went up like sails. He grunted rapidly. Plainly, Habeas did not think a great deal of Ham's new companion.

The feeling seemed to be mutual. The tailless simian seized a stick, rushed at Habeas, and gave the porker a resounding whack. Habeas fled, emitting a series of wild grunts.

That decided Ham. He sat down and laughed, laughed until tears came into his eyes. His predicament was completely forgotten in the glowing light of a great decision.

"I am going to keep that funny looking baboon as a pet," he declared. "Boy, will that burn Monk up. And will it give that pig, Habeas Corpus, something to do besides chew holes in my clothes whenever he can find them."

The tailless simian, having chased Habeas from the vicinity, came ambling back, carrying a stick over one shoulder, gun fashion, Ham struck an attitude, relaxed, scratched his head, then straightened.

"I christen thee Chemistry," he told the simian.

The remarkable looking anthropoid clucked happily as if the new name were perfectly agreeable.

Laughing to himself, Ham struck out again on Monk's trail.

CHEMISTRY FOLLOWED Ham closely. When the jungle floor became tough going, Chemistry took to the trees, but still kept close, swinging along easily.

"Come down here," Ham directed.

Chemistry only sat on a limb and looked stubborn. Ham gave it up and listened. There was no sound. Strangely enough, the feeling that unseen eyes were watching him still persisted. Despite the heat, he shivered slightly. Afraid of nothing he could see the dapper lawyer was nevertheless experiencing vague misgivings, feelings which he knew, having studied psychology, must be a result of the instinctive fear of the unknown, handed down from ancestors who had lived in such jungles perhaps millions of years ago.

Ham shook himself violently as if to rid himself of the fear, then called loudly to the ape, Chemistry. The homely simian was a companion at least.

Instead of coming out of his tree, Chemistry abruptly began to chatter amiably, then swung forward at a rapid pace. Ham, for no good reason that he could explain, took out in pursuit. Swinging overhead, unhampered by clinging vines and brush, Chemistry made the better time. Occasionally he disappeared almost entirely. Ham expressed unkind opinions of Chemistry under his breath. He picked up a short stick. It would be just as well if Chemistry, at this point, learned some discipline.

Something appeared ahead. In the vague light, it looked like Chemistry. Ham let fly with his small club.

"O-o-ow," howled a familiar voice. "Who done that?"

"Monk," Ham called, "it's me!"

"It would be," Monk said disgustedly. "Fine business, throwin' clubs at me. It's a wonder I didn't shoot you."

"Didn't know it was you," Ham snapped, and added so

as not to be misunderstood, "If I had, I'd have thrown a bigger club."

"Who'd you think it was?" Monk growled.

"Chemistry," Ham said and burst into laughter.

"Chemistry?" Monk exploded. Then he eyed Ham intensely. "You gone crazy?"

A frightened squealing from Habeas Corpus interrupted them. Both men wheeled, ran a few paces through the jungle, and came upon a strange sight. Chemistry had captured Habeas Corpus. He was holding the pig, and diligently searching his hide for sign of interesting vermin.

Monk emitted a roar, picked up the most convenient stick. Ham grasped his hairy arm, restraining him.

"Wait, Monk!" he barked.

"Wait nothing," Monk gritted. "I'll teach that funny lookin' baboon to pick on Habeas!"

"That baboon," Ham snapped, "is Chemistry."

"What?" Monk squawked.

"Chemistry is my new pet," Ham declared. "And striking him is the same as striking me."

Just what action Monk would have taken never did develop, for at that moment Habeas managed to bite Chemistry, an expedient which resulted in his escape.

"Chemistry," Ham said, "is some animal, don't you think?"

Monk exhibited symptoms of a spasm.

"Don't tell me you're gonna keep that—that—thing. Why, he looks like nothing else on this green earth."

"I mistook him for you at first," Ham said pointedly.

Monk squawled, "I won't stand for it."

"You'll not only stand for it," Ham retorted. "You'll like it."

Habeas shoved his nose out of the jungle. Chemistry jumped at the pig. Habeas hastily took flight.

Monk began rolling up his sleeves.

"That blasted thing don't go with us," he said. "If I gotta, I'll take both you and your baboon apart——"

Chemistry emitted a sudden weird squeaking sound and leaped toward Ham. He crouched beside the dapper lawyer, knuckles resting on the ground, little eyes roving nervously over the surrounding jungle. He was scared. An instant later, Habeas Corpus scuttled out of the undergrowth and stopped near Monk's feet.

"Blazes!" Monk breathed. "Somethin's around here."

They both carried rifles which they had taken from their late guards. They lifted these weapons, waited, listened.

"Whatcha reckon it is?" whispered Monk.

Ham shook his head, and, in a whisper equally as thin,

said. "Don't know. But maybe——" He broke off suddenly.

There came a dull noise, a whistle and a *plop*.

HAM HAD BEEN standing beside a tree. He ducked wildly, slamming flat upon the ground. An inch from where his neck had been, in the bole of the tree, there quivered a tiny, feathered dart.

"Poisoned arrow!" Monk bellowed angrily. He started to leap forward.

"Don't," Ham yelled. "They may be all around us."

Monk halted, stood perfectly still, rifle ready. There was intense silence. Chemistry broke it with a shrill, almost human cry. The unusual simian leaped, wrapped small, hairy arms around Ham's head.

Ham later decided that Chemistry had made a gesture at protecting him—at least so he took occasion to assure Monk; but at the moment, all that Ham could make out was that Chemistry's embrace was keeping him from seeing.

"Blazes!" Monk barked suddenly, somewhat horribly.

Ham freed himself from Chemistry's embrace. He had been blinded for only a moment; but unpleasant things had happened in that interval.

Completely surrounding them, having materialized like ghosts, stood a ring of natives. These were small men, somewhat wizened in their faces. In their hands was the deadly blowgun used by the uncivilized dwellers in these jungles.

"Don't start shooting," Ham gasped.

"Think I'm a sucker?" Monk growled. "We ain't got enough shells to take even a fourth of these little guys."

Chapter 14

MORE TO DIE

A NATIVE, somewhat taller and a bit more intelligent looking than the rest, stepped forward. He wore a fierce scowl, and he jabbed his arms several times at Chemistry. Then he spoke suddenly, rapidly.

The native's rattling jargon left Monk's face blank.

"He says to drop our weapons," Ham told the homely chemist, and let his own rifle slip from his hand.

"Good night," Monk grunted. "What language is he talkin'?"

"Listen closely," Ham retorted. "If you can't pick out enough words to give you the meaning, you're as dumb as you look."

The native leader was cackling again. Monk listened intently. From an expression of deepest gloom his features changed to radiance, almost joyful.

"Mayan!" he exploded. "It's not the same Mayan language we know, but it's Mayan."

"Right," Ham agreed.

"Then we're among friends," Monk chortled.

The leader of the natives was barking again. His syllables were rapid, explosive. He lunged suddenly, and captured Chemistry. The homely simian chattered and squeaked but did not struggle violently. In fact, Chemistry seemed familiar with their captors.

Men stepped forward, surrounded Monk and Ham and seized them firmly.

"Friends, did you say?" Ham asked Monk sardonically. "Oh, yes, you can notice it very plainly."

Monk scowled first at Ham, then at Chemistry.

"It was that blasted thing you picked as a pet," he declared. "It squawked and hollered and these guys heard it. That's how they found us."

The natives were chattering volubly now.

"Listen," Ham told Monk.

Monk strained his ears, an intense pucker on his brow. He could pick up quite a few words.

"Chemistry seems to be their sacred ape or somethin', as near as I can make out," Monk grunted.

"Exactly," Ham said. "And that is why our lives have

been spared. The sacred ape was friendly with us. That's why they spared us."

"You made that last up," Monk accused. "They didn't say nothin' of the kind."

The argument was broken up by their captors. Ropes made of twisted vines were wrapped around their chests, imprisoning their arms. Neither Monk nor Ham attempted to escape. Not only would it have been useless but probably fatal. Those blowguns and poisoned darts were not things to be trifled with.

Ham now spoke attempting to use the guttural jargon of the natives. They seemed to understand him, but they did not give him the courtesy of an answer. The leader of the little men only shrugged his shoulders.

"If Doc were only with us," Monk grumbled, "I'll bet he could get some action."

FOUR HOURS LATER, Monk and Ham were in no better position. They were very near the exhaustion point. Their little captors had kept traveling at full speed, and had seemed not greatly affected by the terrific heat, whereas Monk and Ham had all but melted down.

Chemistry and Habeas Corpus were still having their difficulties. Chemistry, long arms trailing, stalked along keeping close to Ham, only separating himself from the dapper lawyer to set off in pursuit of Habeas at intervals.

A subtle change began coming over the small natives and it was not induced by their frequent glances at the sun which was flirting with the horizon and giving promise of the coolness of night.

The reason for their excitement became evident a moment later. They were nearing a village. It was obviously a temporary settlement. Bamboo was the principal structural material of the huts. The roofs were thatched, and the floors consisted of platforms a few feet off the ground, this latter structural detail no doubt an expedient to discourage snakes and small animals. None of the huts had walls.

The leader of the natives jabbered. Small but strong hands seized Monk and Ham, propelled them toward a hut which was in the approximate mathematical center of the village.

"Notice anything strange?" Monk whispered.

"Yes." Ham nodded. "There isn't a woman about the place. This is purely a war party."

"A war party of the Inca in Gray, señor," interrupted a new voice in Spanish. It was not a strange voice. They had heard it before. Both Monk and Ham started, spun.

105

Standing beside one of the jungle huts was a man—one of the gang which had captured them when they got out of the crashed dirigible. This fellow made a small gesture. Several other men appeared. These, too, had been members of the party from which Monk and Ham had escaped.

"You are surprised, señores?" a man queried.

"Bugs on you," Monk growled.

The man showed them his teeth.

"You will wait here for a time," he said. "Shortly you will be joined by Doc Savage."

Monk started. "What's that?"

"The great Doc Savage will be with you before long," said the other. "The Inca in Gray has planned it thus, and the plans of the Inca in Gray have a way of working."

"What do you mean?" Monk growled.

"Shut up, Monk," said Ham. "Don't give him the satisfaction of being able to stand there and brag."

Monk and Ham were conducted to a hut, one side of which was shaded by a curtain formed by stacking large palm fronds. This curtain prevented their seeing inside the hut. Their wrists and ankles were bound. They were lifted, tossed onto the upraised floor.

"Good evening, señores," said a weary feminine voice.

Monk turned his head, found himself looking at one of the most beautiful young women he had ever seen. She was tied as securely as were Ham and himself.

"Who are you?" the homely chemist exploded.

"Señorita Anita Carcetas," said the young woman, who was obviously a prisoner.

MONK GAVE EVERY inclination of a man temporarily stunned.

"The daughter of the president of Santa Amoza," the homely chemist blurted.

"Yes," said the young woman. "And you?"

Monk took another look at the young woman and this had the effect of getting his voice. Monk was very susceptible to feminine beauty; and it was Ham, a little less vulnerable, who spoke.

"The missing link here is Colonel Andrew Blodgett Mayfair, better known as Monk," he said. "I am Major General Theodore Marley Brooks, although I am usually called Ham, a nickname I do not like. We are associated with Doc Savage."

The girl was seized with sudden excitement.

"Then Doc Savage is in Santa Amoza?" she gasped.

"Or Delezon," Ham admitted. "We do not know for sure where he is."

The young woman strove to sit erect, but failed.

"You think he will be able to aid us in our present predicament?" she asked.

"Of course he will," declared Ham, knowing that was the proper thing to say.

Monk had discovered that, if he took his eyes from the girl's attractive features, his voice would return. He did so and asked a question.

"Will you tell us," he requested, "what this is all about?"

The girl nodded and spoke swiftly. Words fairly poured from her lips. She told them about the depredations of the Inca in Gray, dwelt upon the mystery behind the sinister master mind's manipulations. She sketched briefly some of the rather hideous crimes committed by the Inca in Gray.

In particular did she describe the fantastic death of the gray dust.

Monk took this all in with great interest. It was their first opportunity, incidentally, to receive a general story of what was behind the affair. Both Monk and Ham nodded comprehension.

"The Inca in Gray has been trying to get us out of the way," Monk said.

"And doing fairly well at it," Ham added.

A faint noise came from outside the hut, from the jungle near by, in fact, a small scurrying sound. Monk's head came up but he could not see what made the noise.

"What about this death of the gray dust?" Ham asked the girl.

The young woman shuddered. "It's—it's horrible. I saw one victim of it. There was nothing to show where the dust came from, how it got there. It was simply there. The expression on the dead man's face—he must have perished horribly." She shuddered several times.

The scurrying and fluttering in the brush broke out again. There was a shrill squeal. Monk lunged against his bonds, fighting to free himself, but getting nowhere.

"They're tryin' to catch Habeas," he groaned.

The squealing and grunting became louder, as did the smashing about in the brush.

"Get heem!" yelled a voice in bad English.

Habeas Corpus dived into the hut, took shelter behind Monk. An instant later Chemistry lumbered in, grabbed Habeas and he held the shote in close embrace.

The pig hunters now appeared. They were the white men.

A few of the natives were with them. They approached Habeas purposefully.

But the natives got between the white men and Chemistry and Habeas. They jabbered excitedly.

Ham listened to the cackling conversation, then glanced at Monk, panted, "Get that."

"Yeah," Monk growled. "They say your dang baboon obviously don't want Habeas hurt. So therefore these other guys have got to leave Habeas alone."

"Chemistry," Ham said, "has probably saved Habeas' life."

"I hate to admit it," Monk mumbled. "But I believe you're right."

There was tension for a few moments, the white men plainly angered at the objections of the natives. The fact that they were greatly outnumbered was something they evidently kept in mind. They backed down, shrugging, showing forced grins.

Habeas showed his gratitude for being saved by biting Chemistry's rather humanlike big toe, which made it necessary for the pig to flee wildly into the jungle.

"Habeas," Ham said, "has about the same disposition as the guy that owns him."

It must have been half an hour later, and the sun was nearly down, when the arrival of a messenger was observed. This fellow spoke rapidly. There was a hum of grim excitement. Natives and white men approached the hut where the prisoners lay.

The fellow who could speak Spanish, bad English, came forward and addressed the captives.

"Word has come from our master, The Inca in Gray," the man said. "You are to be consigned to pits."

Monk looked puzzled, eyed Ham, demanded, "What does he mean—pits?"

The girl, Señorita Anita Carcetas, emitted a short strangled cry. "The ant pit."

"Huh?" Monk eyed her.

"You—you have heard of it," she choked. "A pit—ants—honey——"

Hardened though he was, Monk felt himself grow chilly. He had heard of that method of torture, one used by only the most ferocious of barbarians. It was a slow horrible thing, incredibly cruel. It kept a man alive hour after hour, while he was being literally eaten alive.

Ham had evidently heard about the ant pits, too. Pallor was on his not unhandsome features. But he said nothing.

Rough hands seized the prisoners, yanked them to their feet, pulled them into the red light of the dusk. Monk saw that the girl was being brought along also.

"Hey!" he bellowed. "You gonna do that to a woman?"

"It is the word of the Inca in Gray," said the white man.

But, at this time, the messenger thrust himself forward. He spoke volubly and vehemently.

As a result of the messenger's exhortations, the girl was separated from the other two prisoners, and placed back on the raised hut floor.

The Inca in Gray, it seemed, had not only not ordered her death, but had given specific instructions that she be kept alive. Monk and Ham were marched away.

"Adios," the girl called after them in a voice that she tried to keep firm. "You are as I imagined Doc Savage's men would be—very brave."

"This is gonna come out all right," Monk managed to shout back at her.

They came to a clearing. This was not large, but was absolutely bare, and it was hot, insufferably hot, although the sun had all but disappeared.

The torture pit was in the center of this clearing. Men who had gone ahead were scooping it out. There was nothing particularly terrible or ominous about its appearance, it being merely a shallow hole dug in the baked ground.

Stout pegs were driven into the bottom of the pit when it was completed.

Rough hands seized Monk and Ham, shoved them down into the depression. They were shoved flat. Their ankles and wrists were untied, then tied again, this time to the stakes. They now lay on their backs, spread-eagled, helpless.

The leader of the white men stood at the pit edge. He seized a short spear from one of the natives. This did not have a poisoned tip. He flicked it down. It came so close to Monk that it nicked the flesh of one arm. The homely chemist gave no sign.

"*Diablo*," howled the white man. "Thees ees no essport. Bring on thees honey."

Small natives appeared carrying jars. These held the honey. Streams of the stuff were poured back and forth across Monk and Ham, and up and down the sides of the pit.

"You understand what thees ees for?" asked the white man who spoke bad English. The fellow's face was a grinning, hideous mask. It contrasted starkly with the visage of the little natives.

The white man was enjoying this. The natives were not.

The men carrying the honey jars now walked away through the jungle, streaming the sweetish substance after them, leaving trail.

HAM LOOKED at the homely Monk and demanded, "Know anything about ants?"

"No," said Monk. "And I don't care about starting my education now."

The white man with the sadistic complex laughed at them.

"You will learn much about ants," he said. "They like honey. They will follow this trail. They will come upon something they also like—live meat."

The little men came back with the honey jars empty and grunted that they distributed the stuff in long lines through the jungle, where it was almost certain to be encountered by ants.

The white man growled an order, and they all marched away.

Monk ruminated aloud, "Wonder what kind of ants they got down here?"

"Army ants," Ham told him. "I've read about them. They eat everything. They march over you. They cover your whole body. You know how one ant stings when it bites you. Well, thousands of them——"

"You can save the rest of that," Monk told him. "I got an imagination of my own."

There was silence. It was broken once by the rumble of a jungle drum, close at hand. Evidently, the small natives were signaling in this fashion. A few minutes later, from the infinite distance, another drum rumbled. The sounds were throbbing and seemed to adhere to no particular pattern, but both Monk and Ham knew that the sounds conveyed a message. It was always mysterious, these drum languages of the jungle people. White men seldom fathomed them.

"Look," Ham barked suddenly.

It seemed they had been there for hours, yet it was not yet intensely dark, which meant that not a great deal of time had passed, since twilight did not last long in the tropics.

A single ant was crawling around the edge of the pit, following the honey. It worked downward slowly, seeming to have no particular idea. It came close to the two bound captives.

Monk, with his hairy fingers, managed to pick up a small quantity of dirt. He flung it at the ant. The insect

110 .

scurried away. It seemed to have a purpose now. It went directly over the edge of the pit and disappeared.

"You made a wrong move then," Ham told Monk.

"Why?" the homely chemist demanded.

"Did you ever read anything about these army ants?" Ham demanded.

"No," Monk said.

"They have ant scouts," Ham told him. "You should have let that insect come close, then made sure that it didn't leave to get its fellows."

Monk wet his lips. He felt suddenly cold. This was strange. For the heat in the little clearing must be terrific. Only a few times in his eventful career had Monk felt as he did now, and always that had been when death was close.

"The Inca in Gray!" Monk mumbled. "Damn him, whoever he is!"

Chapter 15

POLITICS

THE INCA IN GRAY was a cloud that had covered Delezon and Santa Amoza. Invisible this cloud, true, but so real that it had touched every citizen of the two republics. The Inca in Gray had become a symbol of terror, just as the bat is the symbol of the night. The Inca in Gray was as symbolic of death as the skull and crossbones. Yet none knew what he—if the Inca in Gray was a man—thought. Never was motive or goal cloaked in more diabolic mystery.

General Fernanez Vigo was expressing his personal opinion of the Inca in Gray.

"A clever fiend," he said.

Doc Savage, Long Tom said nothing. The bronze man was flying the plane. It was General Vigo's private ship, and it had just taken off in the dusk from an outlying spot in the jungle. The ship, the three men had waited there all afternoon, waiting for darkness.

The waiting had puzzled General Vigo. He had asked questions about it.

"Our purpose demands that we reach Alcala, capital of Santa Amoza, unobserved," Doc Savage told him.

ALCALA WAS a vaguely phosphorescent haze on the earth below. The haze brightened. Separate lights became discernible although there were not many of these, and, no doubt, they would be extinguished before long, due to fear of air raids.

Doc Savage selected a spot well beyond the outskirts of the city. He evidently remembered it from his previous flight over the metropolis. It was a vegetable field, smooth enough for a landing.

The plane swooped down, three-pointed perfectly. There was only a slight drumming as the wheels bounced over ruts made by vegetable rows. The ship stopped, so perfect was the judgment with which it had been landed, directly in the shadow of a cluster of large trees. It was not likely to be seen there.

"Any houses close?" Long Tom demanded.

"None," Doc Savage replied.

General Vigo growled, "You must know the country around Alcala pretty well."

"Picking up secluded spots such as this," Doc Savage told him, "becomes a habit when you have been in trouble as much as myself."

PRESIDENT CARCETAS, elected chief executive of Santa Amoza, was an old man. He was also a broken man. His spirit was shattered. His morale was at the lowest of ebbs.

This was somewhat surprising, because President Carcetas' past life had been a hectic one, a violent one. He had fought in revolutions, always on the side which he believed to be right. Twice he had been exiled, only to return in triumph, finally to reach this highest position, that of president of his beloved Santa Amoza. He had always been a fair man; but no one had ever accused him of softness or lack of courage. There had been those who claimed he had no soft spot, that he was an iron man.

They had been wrong, and the evidence was before them, if they cared to look. The loss of his daughter had wrecked President Carcetas. It had pulled the plug of the cask of his courage.

President Carcetas sat alone now in his study in the presidential palace. There was a knock at the door and, without looking up, he said, "Come in."

War minister Junio Serrato entered. Serrato's shoulders were back and he walked sprucely. He looked confident, sure of himself. He looked a bit proud also, and there was reason for that. For he was now the Iron Man of Santa Amoza. He was the power behind the throne. If he played his cards right, he was a power greater than the throne.

"The executive committee is holding a special night meeting," he said. "They await your presence."

President Carcetas turned slowly in his chair and looked at the war minister. President Carcetas' eyes were those of an old and beaten man, either that or he was an excellent actor.

"What is the executive committee discussing?" he asked.

"You have forgotten?" war minister Serrato exclaimed, and looked surprised. "It is a matter of financing further purchases of war material. Count Hoffe's company, as you know, has demanded that we strengthen our credit."

President Carcetas seemed to think that over in a semi-detached way. He nodded slowly.

"I will be there shortly," he said.

War minister Serrato hesitated, then shrugged elaborately. "Very well," he said and went out.

President Carcetas took his head in his hands and sat there. He might have been engaged in deep thought. Once he got up and went to a small mirror, examined himself.

The lights went out.

The lights were out all over the presidential palace, in fact. There was not much confusion at first. Then guards began to scamper around, searching for the source of the trouble. Flunkies ran here and there.

Finally the light came on.

An orderly ran to the door of President Carcetas' office, knocked, was bidden to enter, and did so.

"I wished to make sure that your excellency was safe," he said.

"Thank you," said President Carcetas.

President Carcetas now sat before the desk. About his shoulders was a long cape which he wore on state occasions, and which had been hanging on an ornamental tree near the door. This cape was very long; it was crimson lined; and bore only a single decoration, a design which indicated the wearer was supreme commander of the armies of Santa Amoza. That ornament was a lie as far as present conditions went, for war minister Serrato was really the one who led the armies.

The orderly departed.

President Carcetas now did a strange thing. He went to the mirror again, began to examine his own features, exactly as he had been doing when the lights went off. He did not seem to be satisfied. He drew from his clothing a pencil of the type used by actors. With this he carefully added a line to his countenance.

President Carcetas was deliberately making himself look older.

Satisfied, he turned out the lights and left the presidential mansion.

THE EXTRAORDINARY meeting of the executive committee of Santa Amoza was in full progress. This actually meant that the full government was functioning. Santa Amoza had a parliament, with the conventional upper and lower houses, but this was not in session now; and, when it was not in session, governmental functions, even those of extraordinary nature, were handled by the executive committee. There was an air of grimness over the place.

Arrayed around the room were military guards—and three spectators. The spectators were Ace Jackson, Count Hoffe, and the oil man, Don Kurrell.

War minister Serrato had the speaking platform. He

had a harsh, rasping voice such as a fighting man might be expected to have.

"I have just come from President Carcetas," the war minister was saying. "He will join us shortly, but, before he comes, I wish to make a request of you gentlemen. President Carcetas has just suffered a great shock. The misfortune to his daughter has been almost more than he could bear. He is, I deeply regret to say, not himself. His condition is something that you men can understand. I know you gentlemen, understanding this, will make the proper allowances."

A clever man was war minister Serrato. He knew that President Carcetas was dearly beloved. He had many friends. These friends would be quick to spring upon any one whom they suspected of opposing the president, or conspiring to take away his authority. War minister Serrato was by far too clever a man to antagonize those friends, especially if he could gain his ends by exercising the proper amount of guile.

There was a stir at the entrance. All eyes went in that direction. Many kindly smiles came on weary faces.

"President Carcetas," some one breathed.

President Carcetas came forward, still encased in the long gray robe. He walked slowly as if he bore an infinite burden, and he did not remove the cloak.

He walked straight to the speakers' platform, mounted it, faced the audience and lifted his arms, commanding attention. He began to speak in excellent, distinct Spanish. He was noted as an orator. Never had he spoken in a manner that carried more weight.

"I have something to say," he said. "Please listen carefully, for it is very important."

One of those proverbial pin-drop silences followed his words.

"We have been fighting our neighbor republic of Delezon for almost four years," he continued. "Many brave men have died on both sides. The murder of one of our border patrol, presumably by Delezon soldiers, was the cause. It was a case of our honor demanding satisfaction. If there was honor to be avenged, gentlemen, it has been avenged. If there was pride to be assuaged, it has been assuaged. And yet the fighting has gone on and on."

He paused. It was so quiet that no one seemed to be breathing.

"Gentlemen," said President Carcetas, "we have been fools. We have been pawns. We have been like chessmen, played by a sinister master."

War minister Serrato broke the silence.

"What do you mean?"

"That first border killing that started the war was not committed by soldiers of Delezon, there is every reason to believe," said President Carcetas. "It was committed by another, a sinister master mind, who was deliberately scheming to start the war. And he succeeded. That was the first touch of a sinister hand. But it was not the last. Time and again things have happened which have kept the war in progress. This master chess player, this dread monster of greed, who for some unknown purpose of his own has done his best to keep the conflict in progress, is a name well known to most of you."

He paused for the proper dramatic effect.

"I mean the Inca in Gray," he said bluntly.

There was a pronounced murmur from his audience. Men looked at their neighbors. Quite a few lips were moistened.

"The Inca in Gray has been working in Delezon, exactly as he has here in Santa Amoza," continued President Carcetas.

"How do you know that?" demanded war minister Serrato.

Instead of answering, the president of Santa Amoza held up his arms so as to command greater silence.

"I will ask a man to speak to you now who knows conditions in Delezon, as no one else does," he said.

He paused again.

"I present," he said, "General Fernanez Vigo, dictator-general of Delezon."

General Vigo walked from the door to the speakers' platform.

THE SHOCK of the words and the unexpected appearance of General Vigo created much the same effect as would have been secured by a mass electrocution. Eyes and mouths flew open to their widest. A few persons half arose in their chairs. Yet, so general was the shock, that not a move was made to intercept General Vigo.

General Vigo began to speak the instant he was upon the platform.

"We have a common enemy—the Inca in Gray," he said bluntly.

The words were so unexpected, the mere presence of the commander of the enemy forces so astounding, that no one said a word or made a move.

"I am here to demand something, gentlemen," said General Vigo. "I demand a truce. I demand more than that. I demand peace. And I demand your coöperation. We must join hands, and together stamp out the organization of this mysterious monster who calls himself the Inca in Gray."

General Vigo's words carried great weight. Squat, heavy-set, his ugly face set in firm lines, he was a figure to command respect. The very unthinking courage in his manner was also something that impressed.

General Vigo continued speaking.

"This war has been a hideous mistake," he said. "Peaceful neighbors have been turned into bloodthirsty enemies through no fault of their own. I ask you, gentlemen, to coöperate in stamping out this Inca in Gray."

He surveyed them. The startling effrontery of his presence was still holding them spellbound.

"There will be no difficulty over peace terms," he said. "Delezon demands nothing. Further than that, we will do our bit toward making restitution toward those who have lost most in this ill-famed struggle."

It was a very nice speech. It was having its effect. Should General Vigo say a few more words along this line, and he had them all ready to speak, a mass vote might well end the war.

But General Vigo's speech was never finished. Came a scuffle from the door, shrill cries. A man was trying to get in, a wizened, pock-faced fellow who wore civilian clothing. The guards had grabbed him, were holding him.

It was Don Kurrell, the oil man, who acted first. He sprang toward the struggling group. The man who had tried to get in was gasping out something. He had difficulty ejecting the words, for one of the guards had a hand over his mouth.

But Don Kurrell understood what the fellow was trying to say.

Kurrell spun, lifted his voice to a piercing scream that carried to every portion of the committee room.

"You are being tricked," he screamed. "The man who spoke to you first is not President Carcetas."

Every one heard those words. The import of them silenced the uproar which had started.

Don Kurrell bellowed. "Examine the man who looks like President Carcetas. You will find that his hair is not white. It is powdered."

It was war minister Serrato who acted now. He chanced to be standing very close to the man whom they all had taken for President Carcetas. Serrato sprang forward. He was very quick.

Serrato grabbed at the white hair with one hand, snatched at the cloak with the other. The results were illuminating.

117

The hair was indeed made white by powder. And the cloak, coming away from the figure, revealed not the wasted, gaunt form of President Carcetas, but the figure of a bronze giant who obviously had tremendous physical strength.

The bronze man was recognized instantly.

"Doc Savage!" the shout went up.

Chapter 16

FLIGHT AND PURSUIT

TUMULT SEIZED the committee room. Those present were already emotionally tense. They blew up. They went to pieces.

Doc Savage, abandoning any pretense of further impersonation of President Carcetas, spun to General Vigo.

"Look sharp!" rapped the bronze man. "We are in real trouble!"

General Vigo used an expression which he must have gotten from American movies. "You're telling me?"

The mob surged toward them. General Vigo found himself grasped by the arms, but struck about furiously, freed himself and retreated. Doc Savage was beside him. They managed to reach a window which was shuttered. They broke the glass and tore the shutter loose. Guns crashed behind them as they dived through.

"Kill Vigo!" voices screamed behind them. "Kill Doc Savage! They tried to trick us!"

"Find President Carcetas!" other men screamed.

Doc Savage and General Vigo ran. A slight figure joined them almost immediately. It was Long Tom.

"What went wrong?" Long Tom demanded.

"That is somewhat of a mystery," Doc Savage said. "Some one appeared who knew that I was masquerading as President Carcetas. The fellow had the look of one of the Inca in Gray's men. He has been about before."

Long Tom grunted, "But how'd they know about President Carcetas? Nobody saw us grab him in his study. And we left him bound and gagged."

"Some one must have happened up on him," Doc Savage said.

The three dashed down narrow streets, doubling to the right, then to the left. Abruptly, Doc Savage stopped.

"Long Tom, General Vigo," he suggested, "go get President Carcetas. At least see if he has freed himself. Meet me at the plane."

"Right," Long Tom agreed. "But what do you plan?"

It was not often that Doc Savage explained moves which he contemplated; but he did so now.

119

"Don Kurrell," he said, "the fellow acted strangely. In fact, he gave himself away."

"You mean that Don Kurrell is the Inca in Gray?" Long Tom demanded.

Doc Savage did not answer. He was gone into the night. The bronze man moved swiftly, furtively. He took the house-tops and traveled there whenever he could, because it was safest.

He was retracing his steps to the meeting place of the general executive committee.

The bronze man reached the building. There was great excitement in the vicinity. Angry, shouting groups paced about. Doc watched.

He saw no sign of war minister Serrato, Ace Jackson, Don Kurrell, or Count Hoffe.

Then, some five minutes later, he discovered Don Kurrell.

The short oil man was standing on the outskirts of the crowd, unconsciously indulging in his small habit of drawing himself up on tiptoes to seem taller. His eyes were very busy. He was plainly watching proceedings.

Don Kurrell, after a time, wheeled, looked about as if to make sure no one was watching him, then sidled away. He turned into a darkened side street. He walked very rapidly, looking back often.

Don Kurrell, if he were actually trying to ascertain if any one was following him, was a novice at the game. Not once did he observe the shadowy figure that was Doc Savage keeping close tabs on his progress.

DON KURRELL, it was evident, had some very definite destination, and was in a hurry to get there. He confined his pace to a walk only so long as he was in the excitement zone where there was likelihood that soldiers, seeing a running figure, might shoot and ask questions afterward. Once he was clear, Don Kurrell ran. For a small fat man, he had very good wind. He reached the edge of the city without being challenged.

He still ran, down a rutted lane at first, but soon he left the lane to cut across truck farm land which had been cleared from the jungle surrounding Alcala. He covered some three miles.

His final destination proved to be an enormous barn, exactly such a building as might have been found on a pros-perous Missouri farm. The barn looked innocent enough, but appearances are deceiving.

Planes were being wheeled out of the barn. There were

120

three of these ships, cabin jobs. They were of the type which had wings that could be folded back against the fuselage. This explained how three of them could be stored in a barn.

Don Kurrell ran directly to the group about the planes.

Doc Savage, of necessity, used caution in approaching the spot. Before he was close, the wings of the planes had been hinged out in position, and most of the passengers were aboard. Two of the motors had started. A third motor now started.

Doc Savage tensed. For an instant, he seemed on the point of rushing forward.

Then a man threw a lighted flare from one of the planes. This was evidently to furnish a degree of illumination for the take-off. The flare lay on the ground and burned brightly.

It would disclose Doc Savage before he could come near the plane. The bronze man remained where he was. It was the only wise course.

The light also illuminated with remarkable distinctness the features of those seated in the planes' cabins.

Some of the occupants of the three craft were swarthy, evil-faced fellows, plainly satellites of the Inca in Gray.

Some faces in the planes, however, belonged to the last persons who might reasonably have been expected to be seen there.

President Carcetas, Ace Jackson, Count Hoffe, Don Kurrell, all were seated in the planes.

The ships were in motion. The pilots were not unskilled. They took just the proper run, then lifted the ships off, climbed in conservative fashion, and were lost in the night.

The three ships roared away in the direction of Delezon.

LONG TOM and General Vigo were beside General Vigo's private plane where it had been left outside Alcala when Doc Savage joined them.

"We did not find President Carcetas," said Long Tom.

"Some one must have found him and freed him," General Vigo added.

That was no surprise to Doc Savage. With a few crisp sentences he conveyed to General Vigo and Long Tom what he had seen—the three planes, their occupants.

"Ace Jackson was aboard?" Long Tom gulped. "I can't believe it."

General Vigo swore in Spanish.

"I know Count Hoffe personally," he growled. "The man sold munitions to both Delezon and Santa Amoza. But it is hard for me to believe that he was working with the Inca in Gray."

"Ace Jackson was aboard?" Long Tom gulped. "I can't understand this."

"The whole affair is coming to a head," Doc Savage told them. "Come. We have very little time to spare."

They got into the plane, and Doc Savage lifted it into the air. He did not turn on the lights at wing tips and tail, but flew in darkness and flew high. From time to time he used the binoculars, attempting to pick up the planes ahead.

General Vigo's ship was faster than any of the three cabin craft. Its motor was larger, its streamlining better.

"Think we'll catch 'em?" Long Tom mumbled.

The bronze man did not reply. The question did not seem to be one that required an answer.

After they had been in the air some time, Doc Savage levelled a bronze arm. "There."

Long Tom used the binoculars. He employed them for some moments, shaking his head at first; but finally he nodded.

"I see them," he said. "They're heading for the jungle."

Doc Savage got out of the control bucket, motioned Long Tom to take the stick.

"Follow them," the bronze man directed.

Long Tom nodded, and took over the handling of the plane.

Doc Savage went back into the rear. The bronze man opened the metal case which he had gotten from the wrecked dirigible. This held Monk's portable laboratory.

Doc Savage took from a pocket a small object which, unrolled, proved to be the envelope—the waterproof, airproof envelope of rubberized fabric—into which he had, many hours previously, scraped some of the weird gray dust, which always was to be found on the faces of the victims of the Inca in Gray.

The bronze man began to work over the chemical laboratory. His manipulations were complex. General Vigo came back and stared, but could make nothing out of the proceedings, shook his head and returned to help Long Tom watch the planes ahead.

Hours later, it seemed, although the interval could not have been that long, Doc Savage came forward.

"What have you been doing?" Long Tom asked.

The bronze man seemed not to hear. Long Tom did not repeat his question. Doc Savage had a small habit of seeming to go suddenly deaf upon occasions when he was asked questions, which, for reasons of his own, he did not desire to answer.

They flew on.

"Look!" Long Tom pointed. "The three planes are landing."

It was true. The ships, barely distinguishable in the bright moonlight, were coming down.

Doc Savage took over the controls of their own ship. He promptly cut the motor, and began a long, silent glide to the jungle beneath.

Doc Savage selected a clearing almost three miles from where the other three ships had landed, and he came toward it from a direction opposite the spot where the other three ships had descended. It was not likely that they would see him. He was careful in putting the ship down, not making much noise.

The three of them alighted.

"Now what?" asked Long Tom.

General Vigo spoke up before Doc Savage could make an answer. Until this point, General Vigo had played the part of a brave man, but he had had a hectic night, possibly the most eventful one in his existence.

"I balk, señores," he said.

Doc Savage's flake-gold eyes became intent upon General Vigo. "What do you mean?"

"Let me go back to my camp." General Vigo suggested. "We will need help in fighting this Inca in Gray, and I will bring it. I assure you this war will stop. You've shown me things tonight."

"No," the bronze man said.

General Vigo bristled. His face, in the moonlight, became even more ugly.

"Why do you want me with you?" he demanded.

"We may need your assistance," Doc Savage said.

Long Tom, hearing that, suppressed a desire to snort. If any individual on earth was less in need of assistance than Doc Savage, that person would be hard to locate.

Abruptly, Long Tom frowned. Doc Savage wanted General Vigo with them. Could it be the bronze man had learned General Vigo was the Inca in Gray? The bronze man might have proof that fell a little short of absolute certainty. In that case, if Doc's actions in the past were any indication, the bronze man would not reveal his suspicions until they were shown as irrefutable facts.

General Vigo mumbled and muttered to himself.

"I do not like it, señores," he said at last. "But I will go."

They marched; crawled, described it better. They had lights, but it was not wise to show them.

It was not long before Long Tom started thinking of Monk and Ham.

"They're in a jam," he muttered, "even if they're only lost."

Chapter 17

THE GRAY DUST

MONK AND HAM, at that exact moment, were in a predicament, which they would have exchanged gladly for the mere difficulties of being lost in the jungle. The two men lay in the bottom of the torture pit, and the ants were just beginning to arrive. The insects had been a long time coming. That was not strange, and evidently not entirely unexpected to their captors. The wait for the arrival of the ants seemed to be a part of the torture, the mental portion of it. The physical torture was beginning now.

Monk squirmed furiously, gnashed his teeth, as he felt the first terrible bite. He was not gagged, and he could guess the reason why. Their captors—the white men, for the natives seemed none too enthusiastic about the grisly affair—would want to hear his screams of agony.

There was strange excitement back in the native camp. Men shouted. Orders were cried out. Shadowy figures moved through the night, but it was very dark under the jungle foliage where the moonlight did not penetrate.

Monk heard the sounds, and, more to take his mind off his present predicament than anything else, he spoke of them.

"Somethin's happenin'," he said.

Ham was also in agony. Not many of the ants had arrived as yet, but they were coming in a slender stream that was like a living rope crawling down the pit side.

"They probably have scouting parties out in the surrounding brush," Ham said. "They may be changing shifts."

He was wrong. That was apparent a moment later, when men shuffled up to the pit. Among them was the leader of the white men. He scowled down at them.

"Word has come that the Inca in Gray wishes to be present at your deaths," he said.

"Kind of the guy," Monk growled.

The white man laughed. Brittle and harsh, the sound was like glass breaking. "I think I shall stand here and watch you suffer for a while, señores. The runner who brought word of the Inca in Gray's coming said nothing about treating you gently."

And the man did exactly what he threatened. He crouched

on the pit edge, from time to time using a flashlight to watch the work of the ants.

The electric flashlight had a queer effect upon the small natives. Each time the brilliant white beam lashed out, they started back, as if they considered it magic. This amused the white man, and he entertained himself by throwing the glaring rays over the natives themselves, sending them scampering into the brush. However, when he suddenly discovered a tiny poison dart clinging in the leaves beside him, he gave up his fun.

The jungle drums began to thump in the distance, the sound going on and on in monotonous syncopation. The natives listened to it. Then they gathered about the white man, and they chattered, making fierce little faces. Monk and Ham could understand what they said for their speech was an offshoot of ancient Mayan.

"The Inca in Gray is drawing close," was the gist of what the drums were saying.

Monk and Ham were untied, taken out of the pit, the ants carefully brushed off them with leafy twigs. Then they were escorted back toward the little village with its ramshackle, unwalled huts. Bound hand and foot, they were flung upon the floor of the hut in which lay Señorita Anita Carcetas.

The young woman greeted them as if she had never expected to see them alive again.

"The Inca in Gray himself is coming," Monk told her. "Listen."

They could hear sounds, crashing of the brush for the most part, then tramping of feet, and a file of figures came into the clearing. A small fire, perhaps with ceremonial significance, had been lighted in front of the hut. The newcomers filed toward this.

In their lead walked a sinister figure encased in a gray cloak. The Inca in Gray himself!

The night was hot, travel through the jungle rigorous. The Inca in Gray had thrown back the hood of the strange cloak, so that his features were recognizable.

Monk, Ham, Señorita Anita Carcetas, stared. Their eyes came wide, disbelieving.

"The Inca in Gray is—the last person on earth I would have suspected," gasped Señorita Anita Carcetas.

Chapter 18

JUNGLE

Doc Savage was making slow progress through the jungle on the trail of the Inca in Gray. This was not his fault. Alone he would have had no difficulty in traveling at a good speed and eluding any possible natives. Even with Long Tom alone as a companion, their pace would have been much swifter.

General Vigo was the stumbling block. It had been many years since the dictator general had taken such strenuous exercise as this. Travel through the jungle called for tremendous endurance. Time after time, Doc and Long Tom were forced to halt, to wait until Vigo regained breath enough to move on. A worried frown was on Long Tom's unhealthy looking face.

"I'll stay with Vigo, Doc," he suggested. "You go ahead."

Doc Savage shook a negative. "We will stay together."

He did not explain why. There were several reasons, not the smallest of which was that General Vigo and Long Tom, if left alone, probably could not follow the trail made by those who had come from the three airplanes.

Doc was following that trail now, and it was vague, difficult to trace in the darkness. Had there been daylight, the task would have been simplified greatly.

General Vigo complained loudly, *"Amigos,* I am thinking seriously of telling you both to go where they burn brimstone. *I* have enough of this."

"Not so loud," Long Tom hissed angrily.

But the loud voice which General Vigo had used had already done its damage. Long Tom heard no sound from the jungle about them, but he suddenly found the metallic grip of Doc Savage's bronze fingers upon his arm, and was bundled hurriedly and silently to one side. General Vigo, surprised at the rough treatment, tried to object, but found a hand clamp over his mouth and received a thorough shaking, which impressed upon him the necessity for silence.

The three men came to a stop, concealed quite a number of yards from their previous position. They waited, listening.

A faint rustling of underbrush sounded shortly. A few yards ahead was an open space where moonlight filtered through the jungle foliage. Two natives appeared, slipping along silently through this moonlight patch. Each little aboriginal held a short blowpipe in his hand. Darts, poison-tipped, they carried in bamboo sections which had plugs, bottle fashion.

Doc Savage's metallic hand found Long Tom's shoulder in the darkness. The hand squeezed, long and short squeezes which transmitted a message in the Continental Code. The sallow-faced electrical wizard made no response, but the touch of his hand upon Doc Savage's person telegraphed a reply. "O. K."

The little natives stood in the clearing as if they liked the moonlight better than the jungle. They moved about; obviously they had heard General Vigo's voice, knew that quarry was near. One little fellow stopped close to a tree only a few paces from where Doc Savage and his two companions were concealed. The other native moved ahead.

Long Tom grimaced disgustedly in the darkness. By separating, the two little jungle men had complicated things. For, when one was seized, the other might be able to give an alarm. Doc Savage touched Long Tom, telegraphing with his fingers.

Obeying that silently transmitted command, Long Tom leaped, caught the closest native from behind, and snapping his fingers down on the fellow's windpipe, cut off an outcry.

Long Tom had moved swiftly, but his speed was slow motion compared with the bronze man's action. Doc Savage whipped around the edge of the clearing, keeping in shadow, and was suddenly upon the second native. The little brown fellow did not even succeed in turning, nor could he yell. Doc Savage's fingers did something very briefly to the back of the fellow's neck, and he dropped, asleep for the time being.

When Doc Savage returned to Long Tom, the electrical wizard had succeeded in making his own victim senseless.

General Vigo muttered, *"Bueno.* Now they cannot give an alarm——"

Long Tom took hold of General Vigo's throat with both hands.

"You open that trap again, and I'm gonna wring your neck," the electrical wizard said.

General Vigo still had some fight in him. He bristled indignantly, and combat seemed emminent; but a breathed warning from Doc Savage brought them up sharply.

"Listen," said the bronze man.

They listened. Other groups of natives could be heard approaching.

ALL NOISE of the approaching natives suddenly ceased. Long Tom's anxiety increased. General Vigo's bluster was completely broken, and he was remarkably silent, face down. The three men wriggled through the underbrush seeking to escape.

Birds were fluttering about in the jungle, and that itself told the story. The natives had spread, had encircled the spot. Doc, Long Tom and General Vigo were completely surrounded.

A strange, weird cry echoed through the night. It was picked up, repeated until it came from all directions. The little natives called out to each other. The reason for the noise, at first a mystery, became apparent.

A light sprang up in the jungle. It was a torch which had been lighted. Others blazed, dozens, scores of them.

Soon a ring of lighted brands completely surrounded the spot where Doc Savage and the other two lay.

"Thees ees bad," choked General Vigo, forgetting his English in his excitement.

In charge of the natives was the small chief who had headed the party which had captured Monk and Ham. He gave orders quietly, speaking the offshoot of the Mayan language which was the tongue of his people.

"We have them surrounded," he said. "There is no doubt of that."

Warriors, armed and ready, stood behind the men who held the torches. There were hundreds of the natives here, enough of them to annihilate a small army. Yet, they made no effort to advance. In fact, they did not seem at all bloodthirsty.

There was the sound of a man approaching rapidly through the jungle. A native runner appeared. He was breathing heavily.

"The Inca in Gray is sending one of his men with the dust of death," he said.

None of the little brown men showed any enthusiasm at that. They waited. As their firebrands burned up, they replenished them, keeping a ring of brilliant illumination about the place.

A party arrived through the jungle. A man detached from this group of new arrivals and came forward. He was a white man. He could not speak the tongue of the natives, but the latter seemed to know a few words of Spanish, and, with gestures supplementing these Spanish words, the white man managed to convey his wishes.

The white man's party had brought the dust of death. They desired to make use of it.

Some of the torches were now extinguished. The ring of natives began to move. Gently, ominously, their line crept forward. Shadows flitted from tree to tree, from bush to bush, small, innocent-appearing shadows, but each was a tiny man armed with as deadly a weapon as the jungle has ever produced—blowguns. Light from the torches made a red, hideous luminance.

It was General Vigo who first broke under the strain. "Get back, you devils," he growled at the natives.

There was action then. White men detached from the native ring. They charged forward. They held in their hands strange packages, and shortly their figures were lost in the darkness.

No one watching on that occasion could have told just how the death of the gray dust was inflicted. The devilish operation went forward in darkness, silence, except that there were grunts, cries.

After a bit, the white men retreated.

"Eet ees feeneesh," one mumbled in bad English.

THE LITTLE brown dwellers of the jungle seemed to have an unnatural fear of the gray dust, which was not hard to understand. They drew back, listened. But there was no sound, no stirring from the center of their ring. They lighted more of the torches, and, by exchanging shouts, fired their own courage. Then they advanced.

The light of their torches soon shone upon three prone forms. Guttural exclamations came from the little men. They were not pleasurable sounds, and they were certainly not triumphant, as they surveyed the three inert forms.

The leader signaled his little men, and called out, and they kept their distance from the three bodies. They looked upon the three forms with curiosity.

One was a giant, a herculean bronze figure. The second man was pallid, small, rather unimpressive. The third man was a burly and ugly fellow attired in the army uniform of Delezon, a uniform which bore no rank insignia.

But it was not the prone, motionless figures which held attention.

On the face of each was a fine, grayish powder that gave the motionless bodies a horrible aspect. It was plain that even the little aborigines felt an eerie, creeping sensation, for they drew back, exchanging uneasy glances.

"The death of the dust," one mumbled.

"The Inca in Gray," said another, "has taken more victims. In truth, this Inca in Gray has no respect for life."

With one accord the natives retreated. They kept their eyes downcast.

"The three white men are dead," they said. "We might as well return to the camp."

Chapter 19

THE INCA IN GRAY

THE SMALL brown warriors had left no lookouts behind. Had they done so and had the watchers been alert, they might shortly have seen a happening which, no doubt, would have greatly surprised them.

Doc Savage lifted his head as if to listen more intently, then got to his feet.

"They have gone," he said softly.

General Vigo whipped erect. There was a madness in his manner as he wrenched out a handkerchief and brushed furiously at his face getting rid of the gray dust.

Long Tom also seemed uneasy.

"You sure the stuff won't get us after all, Doc?" he demanded.

"The chances are that it will not," the bronze man said. "It would have taken effect before now."

Long Tom began, "Just what is this gray stuff, and just what——"

"We should be moving," Doc Savage cut in.

The bronze man set out through the jungle, following the natives who were returning to their village.

The trail was a hard one, and it was hot, for the night seemed to have brought little coolness to the jungle. Doc Savage and his companions, however, made good time. They were close behind the natives and the white men when they entered the village.

More fires had been lighted in the village. These furnished considerable illumination.

From the muck beside one of the thatched huts a man came toward the new arrivals. Clad in long flowing robes tightly girdled about the waist the figure was rather indistinct, shapeless. The robe was gray. It had a hood with a mask-like attachment that almost completely concealed the features.

The Inca in Gray!

"What have you to report?" asked the Inca in Gray in Spanish.

One of the white killers with the native party replied in the same language.

"There were three of them," he said. "We got them all."

"Who were they?" asked the Inca in Gray.

"Doc Savage," replied the other, "his aide called Long Tom, and the third man was General Vigo."

That the Inca in Gray was astounded was evident, even though none of his features were visible. The folds of the robe shook as if the wearer were trembling uncontrollably.

"Where are their bodies?" the Inca in Gray demanded.

"We let them lay," he was advised.

"Fools!" screamed the figure in the gray gown. "You should have brought them. I will not believe the bronze man is dead before I see his body dismembered before my eyes!"

The spokesman of the killers squirmed uneasily.

"The gray death," he mumbled, "was all over them. We were afraid to carry them."

The Inca in Gray was screaming now, "You could have made litters! You should have brought them! Go back and get them!"

Rage was pouring from the robed figure. Curses roared into the night, curses in the offshoot Mayan, in Spanish, in bad English, and in good English. The Inca in Gray was a master linguist.

The natives quailed fearfully as did the white followers of the Inca in Gray.

They retreated, anxious to return and get the bodies of their three victims.

"Wait!" shrilled the Inca in Gray.

The cloaked figure summoned the others close. Words were exchanged, low voiced words that did not penetrate more than a few yards.

Doc Savage, Long Tom and General Vigo, concealed in the brush near by, failed to catch what was being said. They strained their ears to the utmost, but it was to no avail.

The natives scurried off, accompanied by their white companions.

All seemed very anxious indeed to get the bodies of the three men who were supposed to be dead.

CAREFULLY CONCEALED on the edge of the village, Doc Savage watched the natives as they departed. The voices of the little brown men came clearly in the night. They were frightened. The rage of the strange gray being, who was their master, seemed to appall them.

Doc Savage stirred, coming quietly to his feet. Long Tom and General Vigo also got erect.

"We will try to reach the huts," Doc Savage breathed.

They eased forward. The night was well along, and the

moon was preparing to vanish. Its disappearance would be followed by a thick darkness, and would greatly complicate attempts to move without noise.

They reached the first of the huts. There had been no sound. Over by one of the fires was a small cluster of natives. These were seated or lying on the ground for the most part, evidently tired out by the night's exertions.

Doc Savage reached the largest of the huts. The shadows were almost incredibly dark. Almost nothing could be seen of the interior of the hut. Doc Savage straightened, intending to search the structure.

Came a sudden gasp from behind him. It was General Vigo. The burly, ugly-faced dictator general of Delezon cried out in horror. His fists made sounds as they struck lusty blows. A shrill angry squeaking echoed the blow sounds.

Long Tom had matches in his pocket. He struck one. There was no longer need of furtiveness. The noise had aroused the little brown natives.

General Vigo was engaged in a furious struggle with a very homely tailless monkey. The thing must have come upon him silently in the night and given him a great start.

"Chemistry!" came a voice from inside the hut.

The speaker was Ham. Doc Savage plucked matches from Long Tom's hand, sprang into the hut. He struck one of the matches.

The elevated hut floor was littered with bound human forms. Monk and Ham were both there. There was attractive Señorita Anita Carcetas, and her father, President Carcetas of Santa Amoza. There was war minister Junio Serrato, and there was Count Hoffe, the munitions salesman. Ace Jackson was also a prisoner.

Only Don Kurrell, the oil man, was missing. Doc Savage began wrenching at the bonds which secured the prisoners. These were of stout fiber cord, woven by the natives. They were not weak, yet they snapped under the metallic fingers of the bronze giant as if they had become inexplicably rotten. Monk heaved to his feet, free.

"They got Habeas Corpus tied under the next hut," he howled and dived outside.

The little brown men had scattered from their fires. Grabbing up their blowguns and poisonous darts, they had disappeared from sight.

Monk came back from the adjacent hut, carrying Habeas Corpus by one oversized ear.

There came a small clicking sound. It was very much as if a match had been dropped on a hard concrete floor, but its cause was nothing so harmless as that.

"Poison darts," Doc Savage rapped. "Tear down the thatch roof of the hut. Use it as a shield while we work into the jungle."

The bronze man had freed all the prisoners now. They began tearing the thatch from the hut roof, intending to use it as the bronze man had suggested.

Long Tom voiced a conviction which he had reached.

"Don Kurrell is missing," he said. "That means he's the Inca in Gray."

"But his motives?" gasped Señorita Anita Carcetas.

"Undale!" shouted General Vigo feverishly. "Hurry, hurry, *mi amigos*. We must get away from here."

Then came disaster. It struck so suddenly that the shock of it paralyzed them. From all around the clearing rifles cracked; bullets storming through the thatched roof of the hut forced them flat on the ground. Poisoned darts began to arrive in a deadly rain. There seemed to be scores of enemies about the clearing.

"The Inca in Gray!" Long Tom exploded. "He did not go to find our bodies. He was too clever for that. He figured we might have faked our deaths and would come here, so he spread his men around the place, set a trap."

"Keep down," Doc Savage said. "Keep the thatching over you. The dart will not penetrate it."

Count Hoffe shrieked. "We are trapped! They will kill us!"

"We don't need anybody to tell us about it, brother," Monk growled at him.

"Quiet," Doc Savage said.

They all fell silent.

The bronze man now began to speak, smooth, guttural words that came swiftly from his lips. He was not speaking Spanish or English but the language of ancient Maya, the pure, untainted tongue of the race which is conceded to have once been the most powerful in the Western World.

He was reciting a chant, a chant that was in the nature of a benediction. Centuries ago these same words had been used by the rulers of ancient Maya to address their subjects. The words belonged to the Kulca, the forbidden language, the language which could only be spoken by rulers, by the high sorcerers.

The chant had a remarkable effect. The little brown natives around the clearing had been shouting out, yelling their war cries. Now they fell silent, ominously silent.

General Vigo rumbled, "Say, what is this——"

"Shut up!" Monk admonished him. "Maybe you didn't know it, but Doc was once made a big shot among the Mayans, and ordained a son of Kukulcan, the Feathered

135

Serpent, or something like that. These little brown fellows are Mayans, even if they have slipped a lot from the old days. Listen."

Doc Savage ended his chant. He began to speak straight Mayan.

"You have been used as dupes, Oh men of Maya," the bronze man said loudly, his voice probably carrying to every one of the listeners. "You have been used by this one who calls himself the Inca in Gray, and who is no Inca at all, but a treacherous killer. He has doubtless promised you rewards for your assistance, but have the men of ancient Maya brought forth descendants so weak that they must help the like of this Inca in Gray? Are you dogs to fight in hopes of being thrown a bone?"

The bronze man fell silent, and it was the turn of the little brown men around the clearing to talk. They shouted at each other, excitedly at first, then angrily. The gist of what they were saying was plain from their voice tones alone. They had enough of the Inca in Gray. They had enough of him before this last incident, for that matter.

Came a strangled yell from the edge of the clearing. The hooded figure shot into view, running madly.

"The Inca in Gray!" Long Tom yelled.

"Blades," Monk exploded. "He's coming to us!"

The cloaked, hooded figure arrived. He stripped the covering back from his head, and it was Don Kurrell, the oil man, and he shrieked, "I am not the Inca in Gray! I was only fool enough to help him!"

Don Kurrell stopped. His face was horrible in the faint light that came from the fire on the other side of the clearing.

"I was promised concessions for my oil company, if I aided the Inca in Gray," he blurted. "I'm only small fry!"

General Vigo got up and roared, "Your lies will not save you! Here's where you get justice!"

General Vigo had plucked one of the poisoned darts from the thatch. He lunged, holding the dart point first. Its venomous tip was buried in Don Kurrell's neck.

Don Kurrell screamed and tried to run, but got only a few paces before he fell, in the throes of the sudden hideous death which the little darts brought.

The end of Don Kurrell did not get much attention. Other things were happening.

Doc Savage lunged at General Vigo. The latter retreated.

"It's Vigo!" rapped the bronze man. "He is the Inca in Gray!"

THERE WAS BEDLAM around the clearing edge, screaming, and shouting and shooting. The little brown descendants of ancient Maya had obviously turned on the white followers of the Inca in Gray. They were fighting to the death.

General Vigo fled madly. He had a start of a few yards. That accounted for Doc Savage not overhauling him immediately.

General Vigo demonstrated himself as being perfectly familiar with the huts. He plunged into one, vanishing from sight in the shadows. Doc Savage followed him.

There was silence for a moment after the two figures disappeared, silence that seemed to those in the clearing, despite the uproar of the fight going on all about them and in the jungle, to drag ominously.

A scream sounded then. It was long and penetrating and there was a shake in it, a ripple of utter horror. That scream must have all but taken the vocal cords out of the throat of the one who uttered it.

Monk emitted a howl and rushed for the hut. Ham ran over to the fire, picked up brands for light. He came with the illumination to the hut.

Inside the hut, Doc Savage stood on the raised floor.

General Vigo was slumped on the floor, dead obviously.

Gray dust—the gray dust that was the special death of the Inca in Gray—covered both the features of Doc Savage and General Vigo. Vigo was dead. Doc Savage was quite patently alive. The bronze man stepped out of the hut.

"Keep away," he said, and began brushing the dust off his features.

Monk swallowed several times and managed to gulp, "But why didn't the stuff kill you?"

"The gray dust," Doc Savage said, "is not dust at all. It is a tiny parasite, poisonous, a parasite peculiar to certain portions of this jungle. The little bugs are almost of microscopic size. Actually, they do not bite. They sting, and, strangely enough, after they sting, they die."

"But they didn't get you," Monk persisted.

"Merely because of an anæsthetic which I mixed in the plane, enroute here," Doc Savage explained. "A plentiful application of the stuff on my skin, just before we entered the clearing was a precaution in the event some one should try to use the gray dust. We used it back in the jungle when we were trapped, but the effects of that application had worn off General Vigo. And actually, the gray dust there was only faked, so Vigo was not afraid, even if my mixture had not been effective."

137

Long Tom jabbed an arm at General Vigo. "But why was he playing the part of the Inca in Gray? He was committing depredations on his own side, the same as against Santa Amoza."

"No," Doc Savage said. "You will remember that we saw no proof of any plotting of the Inca in Gray against Delezon. We had merely General Vigo's word for it, and General Vigo, along with the rest, was a consummate liar."

President Carcetas of Santa Amoza put in explosively, "Then General Vigo's aim——"

"—was trying to smash Santa Amoza," Doc Savage said. "He wanted to control both countries. It was a case of greed, coupled with a mind of devilish ingenuity."

There was still noise of fighting around the clearing, but not as much of it as before. It diminished rapidly. Finally it seemed to be in only one spot, one man resisting. That fellow tried to flee through the jungle. Sounds told the story as plainly as if they had been watching. The natives pursued him. The man's one scream was a sound that would be remembered. After that, silence.

Ace Jackson and Señorita Anita Carcetas were a little to one side. They had their arms around each other.

The little brown men began coming out of the jungle, slowly, keeping their eyes downcast, as if they had done something which they regretted. Their attitude was unmistakably friendly.

President Carcetas of Santa Amoza looked at them, said, "The war will now come to an end, of course. General Vigo was the Iron Man of Delezon. No one can carry on in his place, and, in the peace terms, I shall see to it that these little men, these descendants of Maya, are well taken care of for the service they have done this night."

PRESIDENT CARCETAS of Santa Amoza proved to be as good as his word. Delezon, as he had predicted, did go to pieces following the end of General Vigo. Peace terms were easily reached and they provided an ample reservation of Delezon's richest territory for the native descendants of Maya. The little brown men were satisfied. That is what they had been after all the time.

Doc Savage and his aides did little but act in an advisory capacity as peace was restored. Monk and Ham in particular came under the lazy spell of the tropics. This disgusted Ham. He cast about for some way to restore his usual vitality. He hit on an idea.

He had enjoyed the singing of the natives, even when they sang their war songs, so he decided to take up the task of learning to play some of the native instruments. Monk was right with Ham—especially when he saw the young ladies who were willing to teach Ham these melodies.

It was a splendid idea, and it took up the few remaining days of their stay there.

The day before they were to leave Santa Amoza, something happened that moved Monk deeply—and painfully. The chief of the tribe of the little brown descendants of Maya appeared. He brought with him Chemistry, the most remarkable looking sacred monkey.

The little Mayan made a long speech, an involved oration, but the gist of it was that Chemistry was being presented to Ham as a gift, and would Ham accept?

"Will I?" Ham smiled widely. "Chemistry'll be worth his weight in gold, if he does nothing but keep that hog, Habeas, away from me."

Monk watched the gift giving with open mouth. Monk's groan probably disturbed the condors on the Andean mountains.

To the world at large, Doc Savage is a strange, mysterious figure of glistening bronze skin and golden eyes. To his fans he is the greatest adventure hero of all time, whose fantastic exploits are unequaled for hair-raising thrills, breathtaking escapes, blood-curdling excitement!

- [ ] F 3969 THE TERROR IN THE NAVY
- [ ] F 3937 DUST OF DEATH
- [ ] F 3885 THE ANNIHILIST
- [ ] F 3573 THE BRAND OF THE WEREWOLF (50¢)
- [ ] F 3269 FANTASTIC ISLAND (50¢)
- [ ] F 3455 FEAR CAY (50¢)
- [ ] F 3520 LAND OF ALWAYS NIGHT (50¢)
- [ ] F 3574 LAND OF TERROR (50¢)
- [ ] F 3296 MURDER MELODY (50¢)
- [ ] F 3456 QUEST OF QUI (50¢)
- [ ] F 3387 THE RED SKULL (50¢)
- [ ] F 3441 THE SARGASSO OGRE (50¢)
- [ ] F 3340 SPOOK LEGION (50¢)
- [ ] F 3533 THE SECRET IN THE SKY (50¢)
- [ ] F 3584 COLD DEATH (50¢)
- [ ] F 3667 CZAR OF FEAR (50¢)
- [ ] F 3716 FORTRESS OF SOLITUDE (50¢)
- [ ] F 3782 THE GREEN EAGLE (50¢)
- [ ] F 3841 THE DEVIL'S PLAYGROUND (50¢)
- [ ] F 3805 DEATH IN SILVER (50¢)
- [ ] F 3755 THE MYSTERY UNDER THE SEA (50¢)

8 amazing Doc Savage escapades in a boxed set!

- [ ] K5110 The Fantastic Adventures of Doc Savage ($4.00)
- [ ] NOW available from Bantam—A colorful Doc Savage poster—only $1.00 postpaid!

Bantam Books, Inc., Dept. DS, Room 300, 271 Madison Ave., New York, N. Y. 10016

Please send me the merchandise I have indicated.

Name_____

Address_____

City_____State_____Zip Code_____

(Please send check or money order. No currency or C.O.D.'s. Add 10¢ per book on orders of less than 5 books to cover the cost of postage and handling.)

Please allow about four weeks for delivery.   DS-1/69